M000158147

ABOUT THE AUTHOR

When Chris Behrsin isn't out exploring the world, he's behind a keyboard writing tales of dragons and magical lands. Born into the genre through a steady diet of Terry Pratchett, his fiction fuses a love for fantasy and whimsical plots with philosophy and voyages into the worlds of dreams.

You can learn more about his fiction and download two free books at his website, chrisbehrsin.com.

facebook.com/chrisbehrsin

x.com/chrisbehrsin

goodreads.com/cbehrsin

bookbub.com/authors/chris-behrsin

BOOKS BY CHRIS BEHRSIN

DRAGONCAT SERIES

A Cat's Guide to Bonding with Dragons

A Cat's Guide to Meddling with Magic

A Cat's Guide to Saving the Kingdom

A Cat's Guide to Questing for Treasure

A Cat's Guide to Travelling through Portals

A Cat's Guide to Vanquishing Evil

A Cat's Guide to Dreaming of Fairies

A Cat's Guide to Dealing with Destiny

A Cat's Guide to Serving a Warlock (Prequel Novella)

SECICAO BLIGHT SERIES

Sukina's Story (Prequel Novel)

Dragonseer

Dragonseers and Bloodlines

Dragonseers and Automatons

Dragonseers and Evolution

More works available at: https://chrisbehrsin.com

DRAGONCAT BOOK 2

A CAT'S GUIDE
TO MEDDLING WITH
MAGIC

CHRIS
BEHRSIN

WORLD WALKERS PUBLISHING

A Cat's Guide to Meddling with Magic Copyright © 2021 by Chris Behrsin.

All Rights Reserved.

No part of this book may be reproduced in any form or by any electronic or mechanical means including information storage and retrieval systems, without permission in writing from the author. The only exception is by a reviewer, who may quote short excerpts in a review. This book is a work of fiction. Names, characters, places, and incidents either are products of the author's imagination or are used fictitiously. Any resemblance to actual persons, living or dead, events, or locales is entirely coincidental.

Copyediting by Wayne M. Scace
Proofreading by Carol Brandon
Cover Design Layout by Chris Behrsin

ISBN: 979-8-715305-55-8 (paperback)
ISBN: 978-1-915866-07-1 (hardcover)
ISBN: 978-1-915886-13-2 (e-book)

Published by Worldwalkers Publishing Ltd

To Mitzi, a belovedly remembered feline friend.

NEFARIOUS DREAMS

There he was again, his head floating in the sky, his face with blue skin like a cracked eggshell, looking down upon me with grey lifeless eyes. Astravar... The man who brought me into this world; the evil warlock who hated cats and didn't treat us well.

All around me, purple stalks whipped and flailed, sending up a thick purple mist that stretched across the horizon. If I got close to the plants, they could tear my skin – shred it off my very bones.

I stood there, looking up at the head without a body, paralysed. It wasn't that I couldn't run. But if I did run, then he'd just materialise in front of me, with that wicked grin and expression of dire hatred for any living creature in the world. I couldn't escape him.

This land smelled of death and decay, and each time I came here it became worse. At the same time, I had a metallic taste upon my tongue – a taste of raw meat and of being as wild as wild comes.

I watched, and I waited as the words rolled out of his mouth.

"Join me, Dragoncat..."

Then, I opened my own mouth to say something in his own language, but no words came. It was terrible. I didn't belong here.

My stomach burned with hunger, and I felt the urge to hunt down something and slaughter it. A rabbit, perhaps, or something bigger. Something that would pose a challenge for a great mighty Bengal like me.

It wasn't right. I had to wake up from this dream. I didn't belong here. If I stayed here too long, he'd consume my soul and I'd become feral.

"Join me, Dragoncat..." he said again. "You know it is your destiny."

But I'd promised myself, and I'd promised Salanraja, that I wouldn't let him talk to me for long enough to drag me over to the other side. So, though my muscles wouldn't let me, I tried to move my limbs and stand up. Not in this world, but back in the real world – the world of the living. Even if it wasn't my home.

I tried to open my eyes, but I couldn't. Astravar had too much of a hold on me. If I didn't do something, I'd never wake up again.

I turned to see a strange girl in a long chiffon dress. She looked like a young teenager, with long straight and platinum blonde hair. She rolled her gaze down towards me, and it was then that I noticed her red eyes, the irises looking as if they were burning.

"Wake up," she said.

It was Déjà vu. I'd met her many times, I was sure. But I couldn't place where I'd seen her last.

"I said, wake up!"

My eyelids shot open, and a sudden shudder ran down my spine. A bright white light filled my vision, which soon faded to show a world I knew well enough. It wasn't quite the world I wanted to live in.

But I was much safer here than in Astravar's domain.

WHERE IS PERSIA?

Dawn had already broken, and warm light streamed through the gauze curtains of Aleam's abode. I lay on Aleam's sofa, nestled into the warmth of Ta'ra's furry chest, my mouth now dry and a bitter ferric tang on my tongue. Aleam slept in the next room, the door ajar from where his soft snores emanated.

I stirred, and Ta'ra pushed me away with her feet. I leapt down to the cold stone floor, and I yawned. I went over to lap up some water, imagining it was the soft taste of milk that rolled over my tongue. After that, I wolfed down some dried mackerel, working my way around the thin bones.

How I missed those days of comfort and freedom in South Wales. Now, stuck in the kingdom of Illumine, I imagined I'd never return home. But at least I was safe and not trapped in some warlock's abode as he tried to coerce me into executing his nefarious plans.

"*The dreams again?*" my dragon, Salanraja, asked in my mind. I'd come into this world through a portal created by Astravar, and after escaping I'd stumbled upon Dragonsbond Academy and bonded with her.

"*Every night, now, it seems,*" I replied. "*Why can't that warlock just go back to playing with his crystals and leave me alone?*"

Salanraja hesitated. "*I'm dreaming of him recently too, remember. He's clearly up to something.*"

"*If his demon Maine Coon isn't enough for him, then he can summon another cat from another dimension. Maybe a good Persian would be stupid enough to do his bidding.*"

"*A what?*"

"*A Persian. You know... from Persia?*"

"*Where?*"

I lowered my head. "*I don't know, exactly. Never been there.*"

"*You're an odd one,*" Salanraja said. "*I keep saying it, but I really, really think it's time to tell the Council about your dreams.*"

"*I'll tell them when I'm good and ready... In other words, when I consider them to be a threat.*"

"*Suit yourself...*" Salanraja said, and her voice cut out of my mind. She didn't sound pleased with my decision.

Since Salanraja had learned of my dreams of Astravar, she'd started nagging that I should go to the Council of Three about them. But, in all honesty, I didn't think the Council would be too pleased to hear of them. The Council of Three consisted of the three humans and three dragons who ran this place – three rather than six, because each human was bonded with a dragon.

Last time I'd told them something about Astravar, they'd pinned me up in the air with their magic, probed around inside my head, and then sent me on a near death mission against a bone dragon and one of Astravar's elusive Manipulators. It wasn't so much that I was afraid of what the Council would do to me, but rather that they'd order me to go out and do something about it.

It had been a good month since I defeated Astravar's demon

dragon, and I really didn't want to have to face the evil warlock again. I also didn't want to have to encounter my nemesis, his pet demon Maine Coon.

There came a mewling sound from the sofa, and Ta'ra woke up. She looked down at me, blinked, and then stretched herself on all fours. At the moment, she was the same size as me, but she could change her size whenever she wished. She hadn't done this, though, for quite a while.

She jumped down on the floor, then she strolled over to her food bowl. When she got there, she turned to me and growled. "Ben, you ate my food," she said, and she arched her back, hackles shooting up out of it.

"I did not," I replied. "I've been good, and I only touched my own bowl."

"Then where did it go?"

"I don't know. You must have eaten it." I really was telling the truth. But Ta'ra had seemed a little forgetful as of late.

"Liar!"

She looked like she wanted to pounce, and I readied myself for a fight.

"What is this commotion about?" Aleam asked from the bedroom door. He wore his nightgown and sleeping cap and looked like he'd not slept all night.

Ta'ra turned to him. "He stole my food."

"I did not."

"Did so!"

I groaned, and Aleam sighed at the same time. His gaze jerked from me to Ta'ra, and then he shook his head. "There's plenty more mackerel where that came from, Ta'ra. Though I saw you eating something last night while I was up working on the cure."

He hobbled over to us, leaning on his staff for support, picked up Ta'ra's bowl, took it over to the cupboard, and opened it. As he dished out more minced mackerel from a larger bowl, there came a knock on the main door.

"Come in," Aleam shouted. "We're all awake now."

The door opened to reveal Rine standing there. He wasn't as spotty as when I'd first met him. I guessed it was because he was kissing Bellari less.

"Initiate Rine," Aleam said. "What can we do for you this fine morning?"

He scanned the room, and then he noticed me staring back up at him on the floor. "There you are, Ben. I thought you might be sleeping in Salanraja's chambers."

But that's what so many humans fail to understand. One thing that's great about being a cat, is that you have complete liberty about where you sleep. In truth, it's also entirely political. The more you endear someone to you, the more likely they are to give you food.

Which is why, in South Wales, I chose to sleep in the master's bedroom most of the time. They were the ones with access to the food.

Back in Dragonsbond Academy, I had multiple subjects I needed to keep on my side. The first was Salanraja, the ruby dragon I'd bonded to. I'm not sure she appreciated my company that much. But then who was I to judge? In all honesty, I liked sleeping in her chamber, warmed up by the dragonfire boiling in her stomach. It was just like sleeping by the fireplace in the world where I'm from.

Sometimes I also slept in Initiate Rine's room as well, although less and less since his girlfriend, Bellari, had complained that he was getting too many of my hairs on him. She was allergic to me, you see. Although given her temper, I often wondered if she was allergic to everyone but Rine.

For the last few days, I'd slept here, but given Ta'ra's recent outburst, I'd already decided to try somewhere else for a few days.

Right now, though, I couldn't be bothered to explain this all over again to Initiate Rine. "What is it now?" I asked, because the look in his eyes told me he had a task for me he didn't think I'd like.

He gave me a knowing look. "The Council of Three has summoned you," he said. "They want to talk to you about your dreams."

DREAMWATCHER

Winter had come to the Illumine Kingdom, and for the last five days, a thick blanket of snow had settled on the ground. I wasn't human, and so I wasn't foolish enough to want to go out in the snow. Things froze in such conditions, and animals died if they stayed exposed to this stuff too long.

As you've probably gathered, therefore, I don't particularly like snow. In fact, I absolutely hate it. 'Bah humbug to it', as you might say in the human language.

With each step through the snow, I sank into it, leaving my paw prints trailing behind me in two neat lines. Rine's footprints followed a much wonkier pattern beside them. Fortunately, we only had to trudge for a little way before we reached the Council's courtyard, behind which, I'd learned by this point, stood the keep that housed the most important rooms of this castle, including the council room and treasury.

Two snowmen waited for me at the archway leading into the courtyard. Both of them had eyes made of raisins and courgettes as noses. The guards had built these on watch, apparently, and then they had put two helmets on them to make them look like guards. Apparently, they thought it might help scare away the crows.

Rine stopped by the archway and pointed at one snowman. "Handsome fella, isn't he?"

"I have absolutely no opinion of him," I said.

Initiate Rine looked down at me and smiled. "Apparently, Captain Onus decided how he should look."

"Then I've changed my mind. This snowman is much better looking than Captain Onus."

"I thought you'd say that."

I peered around the snowman and looked into the courtyard. The three elders hadn't arrived yet, it seemed, but there was a girl with light blonde hair standing at the bottom of the dais, her back to me. She seemed to be staring up at the crystal, though I couldn't see enough of her to read her expression.

"What exactly does the Council want of me?" I asked. "And what do they know of my dreams?"

Rine tutted and smirked. "Tut, tut, Ben. Been dreaming things you shouldn't?" He gave me a wink.

"I'm not going to tell you about my dreams."

"Why not? I've always wondered what a cat might dream."

"Because they're personal. Why, would you tell me yours?"

Rine gave a curious frown. "I don't see why not."

"Fine, what did you dream last night?"

"Well, I dreamt that..." Rine scratched his chin as his words trailed off. "Actually, you're right, I probably shouldn't tell you any of that at all."

"Typical adolescent boy stuff, then. I can imagine."

"Probably better than dreaming of fish and chicken all day," Rine said.

"That's not all I dream of. I'll have you know that I have very intelligent dreams."

"Yeah, right."

I opened my mouth to say something else, but a tinny female voice shouting out from the other side of the bailey interrupted me.

"Rine, there you are." Rine's girlfriend, Bellari, stepped up to us. Her long blonde hair framed her face which was red, perhaps because of the cold or perhaps because of her allergies to me. "I've been looking everywhere for you. We start our shift in five minutes. Come on, we'll be late."

She tried to pull Rine away, but he broke free from her grasp and turned back to me. "Bellari, I was ordered to deliver him to the Courtyard. The Council told me to keep close to him at all times."

Bellari sighed and stepped around Rine, keeping as far away from me as she could. She peered around the snowman. "Ben," she said. "What are you waiting for? Go on... They want to see you. And the new student's there already."

"New student?" I asked, starting to get curious. I had thought there was something about the girl I'd just seen in the courtyard. I moved towards the archway. As I did, I closed the distance between me and Rine's girlfriend. Bellari backed away and hid behind Rine.

"Ben, I told you to stay away from me. Rine, do something. Oh, that cat, they should never have Initiated him."

Rine shrugged, and then he lifted his staff off his back. It had a blue crystal at the top, glowing slightly, meaning it was full of magic.

"Okay, Ben," he said. "Either you do as you're told, or I play a game of cat cricket. Which will it be?"

Before I'd come to this world, my reaction might have been to run away shrieking. But I knew if I did that, Rine would send an ice-spell from his staff right after me and freeze me on the spot. Frozen, I might make a suitable cricket ball.

I growled deeply, then I slinked towards the archway that led into the courtyard. The student still stood there, now with her head turned slightly so I could see the side of her face. Her skin was white and unblemished, and she couldn't have been older than thirteen, if that. She had long straight platinum blonde hair that cascaded over a fur collar attached to a thick beige coat.

I turned back to Rine, as I caught a gust of cold air that washed away the taste of the morning's meal on my tongue.

"Go," he said again with a sly grin, and he made a low sweeping motion with the bottom of his staff, which glowed blue slightly as it moved.

I mewled, unhappily, and then I walked into the courtyard. The snow here was even thicker than in the bailey, and I hated the sensation of my paws pressing into it. I groaned as I went, then I thought that maybe if I approached the girl, she could pick me up so I wouldn't freeze.

My only other option was to step onto the dais, but if the Council of Three saw me doing that they might turn me into a frog or something and I'd spend the night trying to work out how not to get eaten by a cat.

I stepped up to her brown leather boot, and I meowed.

She looked down at me. "You!"

When I saw her eyes, I immediately shrieked and scuttled behind the dais for cover. Her eyes were red – I could swear they were – and they glowed like embers.

"I've seen you, many times," she said.

"And I've seen you," I rasped back. "Somewhere..." But I couldn't quite put a claw on where.

"It isn't your place to know who I am... But I know you and your dreams all too well."

Her eyes stopped glowing and took on a lifeless grey colour just like Astravar's. I assessed this girl, unsure whether I should flee or stay put. A creaking sound came from my side, and instinctively I fled to the other end of the courtyard.

But it was nothing to be afraid of yet, as the three Driars of the

Council of Three – Driar Yila, Driar Lonamm, and Driar Brigel shuffled onto the dais and took their places by their lecterns. Well, I say nothing to be afraid of, but they were all pretty scary, being powerful magic users and all that.

"Typical Initiate Ben. Always scared of something." Driar Yila bawled out. She was the tallest and thinnest of the three Driars, with long grey hair and a staff that could shoot fire.

I took a deep breath, then I composed myself. I walked back with my head held high towards the dais. "I don't have magic to protect myself, Ma'am. And what do you expect when you leave me to contend with this witch!"

"Seramina is no such thing," Driar Brigel said. He was the only male in the Council of Three – a gentle giant with thick, muscular arms hidden underneath his tunic. "She's our new dreamwatcher among other things. We've been bereft of one for a good ten years."

"What the whiskers is a dreamwatcher?" I asked. Then I remembered myself. "Sir..."

Brigel smiled and glanced at Driar Lonamm, who lowered herself on her stout frame to peer down at me. "Initiate Ben, you promised us you'd inform of all strange going's on. And yet, here you are holding a tremendous secret from us."

"A secret?"

"Your dreams," Driar Yila said. "Your dragon told me all about them... Ben, you must be punished for this. You know the rules. You've risked letting Astravar inside Dragonsbond Academy by not telling us this."

"But it was a dream!"

"It doesn't matter. There are many ways to penetrate a castle. Young one, it appears you still have a lot to learn."

That caused me to stop in my tracks. I felt the rage boil up in my chest all of a sudden, almost as if I had dragonfire burning within.

"Salanraja," I said in my mind. *"You promised you wouldn't say anything to them."*

"Correction," Salanraja said. *"I told you I would give you time to tell them yourself. But once the dreamwatcher told me what had happened in your last dream, I realised I didn't have a choice."*

"And what exactly is a dreamwatcher?"

"Exactly what the name says. She walks around at night watching people's dreams."

"So, when does she sleep?"

"She sleeps as she walks..."

I looked back at the girl who was staring up at the massive crystal above the three Driars as if nothing else existed in the world. Her eyes had that red glow to them again. Another gust of wind came, kicking up the snow around her feet. It whipped her hair into her face, but she didn't even flinch.

The three Driars were watching the girl, each of them with their heads cocked and expressions of curiosity on their faces.

"He's here again," she said. Her mouth moved, but she didn't even blink or change her expression. It was as if she was channelling the words from another dimension.

Driar Lonamm cocked an eyebrow. "Astravar? But who would be sleeping at this time?"

"Not a student," Seramina replied. "The fae. The Cat Sidhe."

"Ta'ra?" I asked.

"She's moving," the girl said. "She's on the walls... With Astravar inside her head."

"Go," Driar Yila shouted out. "Ben, go after her and wake her up at once."

"What, why me?"

"Because you're the only one fast enough," Driar Lonamm said. "Ta'ra is under our protection, and we can't risk losing her to the warlocks. Go!"

I growled at the Driars for making me move in such cold weather, when all I really wanted to do was curl up by Aleam's fireplace and sleep.

"Don't test us, Initiate," Driar Yila said, and she banged the butt of her staff against the floor. That was enough to startle me out of the courtyard. I heard Seramina's feet pattering behind me, but she wasn't as fast as me.

In front, a crow lifted into the air, cawing loudly. It joined a flock of other screeching crows wheeling above the academy. Ta'ra was already on the castle walls, looking up at the flock. She turned to me and yawned with her eyes closed. Then, without opening them, she jumped down off the other side of the wall.

❧ 4 ❧

SLEEPRUNNER

"Ta'ra!" I shouted as I sprinted after her. I jumped up onto the *chemin de ronde*, using the gaps between the stones as pawholds to pull me up. A couple of the archers on watch looked at me disdainfully. Last time I had done this, they had tried to shoot me down with their arrows.

But now they had their bows pointed up at the crows and they were loosing their arrows at them. A couple of crows plummeted from the sky into the moat.

Ta'ra was already emerging from the other side of the moat which must have been freezing at this time of year. I shuddered just thinking of crossing it, but I had no choice. So, I dived right into the water, and I went under for a moment, before I surfaced again on the other side and scrambled up.

I didn't even have time to shake myself off. Ta'ra was already running fast, tracking the flock of crows that were flying above her. The birds seemed to be following a bright purple light that they circled around. Ta'ra also seemed mesmerised by it, because she didn't watch the landscape ahead of her, but rather the flock as she ran.

This meant she should have been easy to catch up to.

But the snow slowed me down a bit. I was a Bengal, descendent of the great Asian leopard cat, and I'm sure my ancestors never had to deal with this disgusting stuff. Ta'ra, however, seemed fleet footed on it. So much so, in fact, that I still had to sprint to have any chance of keeping up with her.

Fortunately, she hadn't tried growing to five times her size or anything like that, because if she did, I was sure she would outpace me.

"Ta'ra... Stop! Wake up! Don't let Astravar into your dreams!" I shouted.

Maybe she could hear me, or even see me in my dreams. But then, although I seemed to vaguely recall another figure in my dreams, I could only vividly remember Astravar.

I was just a couple of spine-spans away from Ta'ra when the crows cackled loudly into the sky above me. They shot down like they had rabies, pecking their beaks into the ground and creating thin dents in the snow. I rolled out of the way of one, which I swear almost speared me right through the head.

They were going crazy. What the whiskers was causing this? Crows don't attack the living. Especially not a mighty creature like a cat.

"*Ben,*" Salanraja called out in my mind. "*Hold on, I'm coming for you.*"

"*I can handle a few birds. I'm a Bengal, descendant of the great mighty—*"

My words were interrupted by a loud roar that cut through the sky and made the ground shudder. A gust of wind came from above, and a shadow passed over me. I raised my head to see Salanraja letting off a jet of flame at the flock, which scattered in the dragon's path. Some of them fell to the ground, and some of them managed to break free and continue to plummet down and attack me.

But Salanraja had given me enough space to continue after Ta'ra who had gained quite a distance on me. I readied myself at a crouch, and then I sprinted at full speed to catch up with her. I overshot a little, and I turned around to see her frozen on the spot.

Her eyelids covered her eyes completely, but still she had her head turned to me, as if she was looking right at me. I tried to move to the side a little, and she tracked my movements with unnerving accuracy.

"Ta'ra, wake up!"

She didn't respond to me in any way. Instead, she turned her head up to the sky, and let out a whining sound as if she was after a fly. The purple light up there floated over to her, and the crows that Salanraja had disrupted had started to gather around it. Salanraja was much further away in the distance, coming in at them for another pass.

"Whiskers," I said. "I'll have to wake you up through more conventional means." I moved in towards her, and I struck out to bat her on the cheek. But she caught my paw and knocked me away with unbecoming strength.

"Ta'ra... It's me... Stop this!"

She growled back at me, her eyelids still sealed shut.

"Ta'ra? What's happened to you? Wake up."

Still nothing. The hackles shot up on the back of my neck as she opened her mouth to hiss at me. She grew to the size of a panther, and then she leapt at me. I rolled out of the way, just missing another crow trying to spear me from the sky.

I considered fleeing, but I knew Ta'ra would outrun me, and so I turned to face her. She launched herself off her haunches to pounce at me. I shrieked as I clawed at her, but she pinned me to the ground, baring her teeth and growling angrily. Her eyes were still fastened shut, and I tried to shriek as loudly as I could to wake her up, but it had no effect.

She stopped then, as if to regard me from behind those sealed eyelids. "How disappointing, Dragoncat," she said. "I would have thought a great mighty Bengal like you would have put up more of a fight. Perhaps, your ancestry isn't as great as you claim."

"Astravar," I said through bared teeth. "Release her..."

"Or what?" Ta'ra asked. Or at least Astravar asked through Ta'ra's mouth.

I said nothing.

"You know, maybe I don't have a need for you after all, Dragoncat. I had forgotten about this specimen whom I'd transformed so long ago. But she could be a useful tool in my plans."

"Let her go!"

"No," Astravar said, and then he brought Ta'ra's mouth down towards my neck. I tried to flinch out of the way, but she had me pinned to the ground with one paw over my chest. I thought that she'd eat me then, but instead she licked me using her long tongue.

It isn't pleasant being licked by a cat, and particularly a big one. The chitin at the back of her tongue, meant for helping to mash up her meals, scratched through to the skin and brought some fur off the side of my face, as if it were sandpaper.

"Oh, what fun this is," Astravar said.

I didn't have a clue where Salanraja was right now, but I really needed her. "*Salanraja, get her off me. She'll kill me!*"

"*I can't,*" she said. "*So sorry.*"

"*Why not?*" I asked, as I squirmed relentlessly under Ta'ra's grasp.

"*Because we have other plans.*"

"*What?*"

I was answered by a roar, and not Salanraja's. It came from the direction of the castle, followed by the sound of great beating wings.

Ta'ra turned towards it, her eyes still fastened shut. I also strained my head to see what we faced.

There was a charcoal dragon, so much smaller than the other dragons I'd seen that I thought it must only be a fledgling. On the back of it sat that weird girl with the flaming red eyes and long straight blonde hair. She carried a staff raised above her head with a glowing white crystal affixed to the top of it.

"That meddling witch," Astravar said through Ta'ra's mouth. "What wasted potential." The Cat Sidhe lifted her paws off me and started to sprint away. Before she could get far, though, Salanraja swooped down from the sky and thudded down on the ground in front of her, blocking her path.

She tried to turn to evade, and a narrow beam of white energy from Seramina's staff hit her on the side of the head. Ta'ra started to run again, but it was like her body didn't want to follow her legs, as if she was physically in battle against herself.

Soon, she skidded to a halt, and then her head turned towards me. Still, her eyes didn't open. "This isn't the end. I will find another way." As she spoke, she shrank until she became a normal cat size again. I was pretty sure that Astravar was trying to reduce her further, maybe as a ploy to steal Ta'ra away.

Another narrow beam of bright white energy came from Seramina's staff, this time hitting Ta'ra right between the eyes. It lasted for a few seconds before her eyes shot open.

I gazed into the bright green eyes of a very confused black cat.

5

LESSONS IN DRUDGERY

Two days later, I was lying, comfortably sleeping, in Salanraja's chamber, nestled up against the warmth from the dragonfire burning in her chest, when the bell rang to signal the start of class. Admittedly, there wasn't much else to do in winter other than studying, and Driar Aleam had pointed out that I had a lot to learn.

The sun hadn't even risen yet. Mind you, I usually liked to wake up when it was still dark. Nights were far better for hunting and sneaking up on your prey while it slept.

I lifted myself up and stretched out, yawning. A crescent moon hung high in the sky, and I looked out at the place that I'd awoken Ta'ra from her dream.

I stalked down the spiral staircase, and onto the cobblestones, everything lit by flaming torches of the kind I really didn't see much of in South Wales. Much of the snow had melted the previous day, reducing it to puddles and slush. Some guards eyed me suspiciously from the walls, and I hissed back up at them to communicate that if they tried shooting me down, the Council of Three would eat them for breakfast.

Astravar's attempt to capture Ta'ra had put the whole of Dragonsbond Academy in lockdown. The Council of Three had ordered the archers on the wall to shoot anything that left on sight. That included cats – especially cats, Driar Yila had said.

Of course, it takes a lot of effort to imprison so many cats in such a large space. You have to make sure every nook and cranny is covered. Which is what the humans did – they greased the walls so me, my brothers, and my sisters couldn't scramble up them, and they put these tall spiky wooden barricades around the staircases leading onto the walls, so high and sharp looking that no cat would dare even try to climb them.

I admit, I did scout the grounds a few times to check for any ways out. But the guards and carpenters here had done their jobs well and sealed the place off tight. Meanwhile, Ta'ra was locked in a small room in the guard's tower, the cats here were now let out into the bailey at all times, instead of being confined to the cattery during the day. If there was one thing Dragonsbond Academy needed right now, it was efficient crow-catchers.

A few of them, including a white cat with pink ears, had gathered around Captain Onus who dangled a ball of wool that apparently resembled a crow from a fishing rod. The white cat was so agile, she leapt up to catch the ball of wool in both her paws, and then pinned it to the ground.

In response, Captain Onus laughed, and he produced a piece of dried beef from his satchel and threw it on the ground in front of the white cat. It looked so delicious.

In a way, I wanted to join in the fun. But I knew I had a classroom to fall asleep in.

Just as the sun began to rise, the bell rang again to remind all of the students not to be late to their allotted lessons, and several throngs of students came out from the dormitory doors on the other side of the bailey. Some of them laughed away in conversation, while others stopped to drink from the water fountain.

I watched the students for a while, looking out for that platinum-blonde haired teenage witch with the power to watch dreams. I couldn't find her anywhere, but then she seemed the type to get to class well before everyone else.

Instead, a familiar voice came from the side of me. "Initiate Ben," it said. "Aww, it's been so long."

I looked up to see one of my favourite students, Ange, looking down at me, smiling a little goofily. She brushed a few strands of short brown hair away from her eyes, and then she leaned down and tickled me under the chin.

"Here, kitty kitty," she said, and she laughed.

"You know, I'm around three times the age of a kitten," I said. "In human terms, I'd be much, much older than you."

"Well, aren't you the wise one?" she said, and she bent down and lifted me up into a nice soft cuddle. "Come on, we'll be late for class."

I liked Ange; I really did. She was one of the few humans in Dragonsbond Academy who seemed to grasp how much we cats deserved pampering. I also still held that she was a much better suitor for Initiate Rine than Bellari. Her perfume, I swear, even had a whiff of catnip in it, which said a lot about her character.

I purred as she carried me along in her warm embrace, keeping her gaze down on me and ignoring the harsh, disapproving stares she got from some of the other students. Really, I don't know why so many of them still hated cats so much. I mean, humans worked the cats like horses here.

Really, it was meant to be the other way around – the cats should have been working the humans. I couldn't get over, sometimes, how messed up this world was.

The bell rang a third time, much louder than the other two.

This was the final warning to get to class, which sent all the students into frenzies of panic.

Ange hurried too, but I didn't mind because I wasn't doing the walking. She waltzed me across the bailey, into the stone corridors, past the kitchen that smelled of herby goose, and into the dusty classroom. She placed me down in a custom-built chair – built higher than all the other chairs – and then she took the seat just next to me. Initiate Rine stumbled in and smiled at Ange, then sat in front of her. Bellari came in shortly afterwards with a red face and sat deliberately three desks away from Rine, letting out an incredibly loud huff as she plonked her bottom down on the stool.

Driar Brigel was the teacher for today. The gentle giant watched the students file in, with his bare arms crossed, showing the thick muscles on his forearms. "Come on, come on, you're all late again. How we're running a military academy here when none of the students are on time, I don't know."

A goose-feather quill lay on the desk in front of me. "Hello Ben," it said to me, and it stood up on its tip, and then dipped itself in the inkwell containing concentrated beetles' blood. The inkwell glowed from within, giving it a blue tint. This wasn't due to the ink, but the white magic crystal inside there that apparently allowed me to put my thoughts to paper. It made a lot of sense really, because in my whole life I've never seen a cat that can write with their paws.

The quill moved over to the aging parchment already on the desk in front of me and inked something down at the top of the page. It didn't matter to me what it said – my crystal had given me the ability to speak languages and not to decipher writing. But then I wasn't going to be the one reading it – it would be our Driar teachers who examined the thoughts that came to my mind which the pen, consequently, knew how to read.

I ignored the pen, scratching away, and turned my attention to the front of the classroom where Driar Brigel had started to deliver his lesson.

Cats aren't meant to sit in classrooms and watch the teacher scratch arcane symbols on the blackboard in different colours of chalk. Though, fortunately, most of the teachers didn't just rely on writing but said things out loud too. The problem was that Driar Brigel, it turned out, had an incredibly boring teacher's voice.

The lesson today was on alteration, or in other words the kind of magic that allows you to change your form. Of course, because the Cat Sidhe, the cause of the lockdown, was on everyone's mind right now, Driar Brigel decided to use her as an example to explain the concept.

Alteration spells were interesting to me, because they always came with a catch. If you turned into something too much, then you eventually became it. It all depended on the power of the crystal and the ability of the caster. Astravar, apparently, had cast a dark alteration spell on Ta'ra, which turned her from fairy to cat. But he'd done something – and no one quite knew what – to make it so that when Ta'ra used her ability to turn back into fairy form, she could only do it for a day, and then she'd turn back into a cat again. Once she'd turned back eight times though, she'd be permanently a cat, because that was the way that alteration worked.

Driar Brigel also surmised that Astravar had cast the spell this way, so he could take advantage of Ta'ra's fairy magic sometimes, but he wouldn't risk her accidentally casting anything when she was in cat form. If she did become problematic, he wouldn't have to deal with her fairy form this way for anything more than eight days.

When Ta'ra took on her final cat form, she would also lose things like the ability to speak the human and fairy languages, and her taste for certain foods. Around me, everyone seemed to shudder when Driar Brigel said this. But I personally didn't see why this was so scary. I mean, it seemed normal not to like things like vegetables and bread and to instead focus on the good stuff like meat and eggs and dairy. Whiskers, humans were so strange.

As Driar Brigel droned on, I found myself less and less able to focus. Alas, although I was curious what Astravar had done to Ta'ra, Driar Brigel's dry voice eventually sent me to sleep.

6

A CALL FOR COURAGE

The wind soughed through the needles in the pine forest all around me, and the ground felt crunchy underfoot. The sun shone down from the sky, adding extra warmth to the heat coming from a roaring fire.

I was expecting to see Astravar in my dream, but he wasn't there, and instead I found myself looking at a massive salmon roasting on a spit. It sent off delicious smells, scented with tarragon and lemon, neither of which I minded, so long as they were only used as mild flavouring.

Salmon, oh how I missed it. There was none of it in this world, and often I wondered if I would taste it ever again. A man was sitting by the fire, wearing a brown cloak. His face wasn't visible through the shadow of his hood, and part of me wondered if I was looking at Astravar. But he didn't smell like Astravar – and trust me, I'd know because that warlock carried the odour of rotten vegetable juice with him wherever he went.

The man didn't move like Astravar either. I watched, and I

waited as he turned the salmon around with a solid branch. I meowed to tell him that I was hungry, and that I hadn't eaten for a long time. But that didn't cause him to stir one bit, almost as if he didn't realise I was there.

Suddenly, there came a rustling from the forest behind me, and I jerked around, expecting to be looking at the sharp teeth of a wolf or something. Nothing was there, only the crackling and the heat coming from the fire behind me.

And a stench, this time of rotting meat coming from behind the fire. Suddenly, the heat disappeared, and everything felt so cold. Day quickly fell to night, and I felt the presence of something much larger than myself behind me. The hackles shot up on the back of my neck, and I turned towards a face three times the size of mine.

I'd seen it on the television, and the Savannah cats back home had told me this beast was almost as dangerous as a hippopotamus. A mane surrounded its yellow face like a picture frame. It regarded me in a characteristically catlike way. Except its catness wasn't like any cats I knew.

A lion – the king of the Savannah. The greatest hunter in the world from which I'd come. The beast that every cat wanted to be.

"Can I have your autograph?" I asked.

The lion didn't give me an answer, or at least an intelligible one. Instead, it opened its mouth and let off both an incredibly smelly and incredibly loud roar – the stench and amplitude of it meant to paralyse, I was sure.

It was then that I noticed that this wasn't any normal lion. It had another head – one of a goat – protruding out of its neck, and a third one coming out of its tail – that of a venomous-looking snake.

I'd never seen anything like it in my life.

I'd had my moment of freeze, and now it was time for either fight or flight, and one of those options seemed much more appealing than the other. I spun around and sprinted off into the forest, not looking back once. I brushed past thorny branches and nettles, but I didn't let the pain from the scratches deter me. As I went, I turned my ears behind me, listening for that beast's footsteps crunching over the forest floor. The wind sounded like voices whispering through the trees, and I was expecting to see Astravar's face at any moment.

Eventually, I came into a clearing, and realised nothing was following me. I spun around, looking for that thing, but it had assumedly decided it didn't want to eat me for supper.

I had emerged in a glade, with a lake stretching out in front of me, the surface as clear as bowl-water. I could see the orange and yellow fishes swimming around as if they didn't have a worry in the world.

But they should have been worried because a cat had just entered their domain. Intently, I studied their movements as I tried to work out how I could catch one while avoiding getting wet.

"*What you need is a good fishing net,*" a voice said to me, and it took me a moment to realise that it hadn't spoken out loud but in my mind. "*Maybe attached to a simple rowing boat.*"

The words sent a shudder down my spine.

Astravar had found his way to me finally, and he was going to try to possess me like he had Ta'ra. But the voice didn't sound like Astravar. Instead, it was female and had a nice soft lilt to it. She sounded much like the mistress back home in South Wales.

I looked up to see a crystal spinning above the water. In it, I could see images of myself kneeling over the side of a rowing boat and chasing fish. I was looking right into the facets of my crystal, meaning that what it was showing was one possible thread of the future. But all of a sudden, I didn't fancy going fishing anymore. I didn't want to get my paws wet.

"It has been a while now, young Ben," the crystal said. *"And what progress have you made in pursuing your destiny?"*

Her question caught me off guard. After defeating Astravar and his demon dragon, I'd been so busy just surviving in this world, that I hadn't really had time to think about any of that 'pursuing my destiny' palaver.

"I've used my gift of language to talk to a lot of people," I said after a moment. *"And I managed to command a demon dragon and return it to the Seventh Dimension."*

"I do not ask about the past," the crystal said. *"I ask about the present. What are you doing right now to improve yourself and make sure you're on the right path?"*

"Improve myself?"

"We're all on a path of either growth or decay, and your actions now will determine how you will grow."

I thought about it for a moment. *"I'm eating a lot of good food,"* I said. *"That helps me grow and become strong. But if I ate rotten food, I'd surely decay."*

"I'm not talking about your physical form," the crystal said. *"I'm talking about becoming the hero who can face and defeat your nemesis. If you don't become stronger, then the warlocks will destroy all life in all dimensions. This is the fate that I have foretold."*

I groaned. I didn't like the sound of this self-improvement stuff. I'd seen humans do it on television sometimes. It seemed to involve lots of painful stretching and listening to dull and repetitive music.

"What the whiskers do you expect of me? Because right now I'm utterly confused."

"You need to learn courage," the crystal said. *"Or in other words, the ability to circumvent your instinct in the face of fear and keep a level mind. You must face the chimera and win, young Ben. Then, it will be time for your second spell."*

"My second spell?"

But the dream was already fading to white. The fish went first, then the lake, then the ground and the surrounding trees. The crystal blinked out last, leaving me facing a wall of whiteness.

Then I awoke.

7

GOOD EDUCATION

I don't think it was the dream that woke me, but the bell ringing out indicating the start of our lunch break. An immediate commotion exploded from the classroom, as the Initiates all around me leaped up from their desks. They left their parchments and inkwells on the table and made towards the door – creating a bottleneck at the entrance.

"Don't forget your homework," Driar Brigel shouted out as he rubbed his writing off the board. "I expect all parchments back on my desk at this time tomorrow."

No one seemed to hear him. I also had a bit of a problem, as I'd never heard what the homework was. Once Driar Brigel had wiped the board clean, he looked around the classroom and then strolled up towards me.

Ange was still sitting at her desk, her nose buried in her parchment as she wrote down some notes. Driar Brigel looked over her paper, and she glanced up at him, then returned to whatever it was she was studying.

"Always a dedicated student, Initiate Ange," Driar Brigel said.

Ange didn't look up from her parchment. "Just give me a minute, sir."

Driar Brigel smiled. "No problem. You can have as long as you need."

I yawned as he approached and leaned over my desk. He peered down at my paper, a slight gleam in his eye. "Now I wish I could say the same of Initiate Ben. What's this long line, here? It looks like your thoughts went blank for a while. Did you drift off again, Ben?"

I growled. "I'm a cat, what do you expect? We're not meant to do stuff during the day."

"But you still need to study like everyone else. Tell me, what did you learn today?"

"I learned of the dangers of alteration."

Driar Brigel raised an eyebrow. "Oh, and what might they be?"

"Never to get involved with it," I said. "Because I might end up turning into a human or something and never being able to turn back..."

"Or a dog," Driar Brigel said with a chuckle.

I shuddered. "Definitely not a dog. Nothing's worse than turning into one of those."

"Worse than a cockroach?"

"Yes," I said. "At least cockroaches find it easy to hide."

Driar Brigel shook his head. Then, something on the paper seemed to catch his eye. "What's this? Transmutation into a chimera? What were you dreaming, Ben?"

"Nothing."

"Was the warlock there?"

"No..."

The Driar studied me for a moment. "Fine. Just try harder to concentrate. I don't want to have to fail you at the end of the year."

"Yes, sir," I said. The crowd had now dispersed at the door, and so I leapt down to leave Ange to her studies and Driar Brigel to whatever he wanted to do.

"*Bengie,*" Salanraja said in my mind after I was through the door.

"*Yes?*"

"*It appears it's time.*"

"*Time for what?*"

"*I know you had a dream too. The crystal contacted us, and it seems you have a mission from the source of magic itself.*"

I growled, causing a couple of students waltzing down the corridor to jump out of my way and then look at me funny. "*I'm not sure I want to. Besides, we're on lockdown here. We can't leave.*"

I was outside now, weaving my way around the puddles created by the melted slush. The air smelled of wood smoke, and the students had gathered in the bailey, playing a game where each player had a piece of string stretched across the span of their arms. One student would use this to throw an hourglass shaped cut of wood up in the air to be then caught by another student on their string.

The bell rang again, signalling lunch was ready. The students dropped their toys and immediately rushed back into the corridors towards the kitchen. I started to follow them, until Salanraja said, "*You know, I've got a whole cow up here. Roasted by my own breath.*"

My mouth immediately began to water. I mean the food from the kitchens was good, but they'd not had much beef recently, which was exactly what my stomach wanted right then. "*I guess when I visit, you'll be giving me another lecture.*"

"*Beef, Bengie. Just think of the beef!*"

Whiskers, when she put it that way, I couldn't think of anything else. "*Fine, I'm coming.*"

Hence, I made my way towards Salanraja's tower – not quite sprinting, but at least with some urgency in my steps. On the way, I passed a lady with raven black hair spilling down both sides of her face in waves. She wore a black woollen cloak, unbuttoned near the top to reveal a white frilly shirt underneath it. She wasn't a student but looked more to be in her thirties.

"Hello, Ben," she said as I passed. "Fancy seeing you here." She raised her hand to her mouth and giggled.

But my stomach was rumbling too much by this point to pay her much heed. It wasn't until I reached the staircase that I realised I'd never seen her before in Dragonsbond Academy. I turned back to look for her, but she wasn't anywhere to be found.

8

LUNCHING WITH THE DRAGON

Salanraja, as promised, had prepared a delicious feast of flamed beef. My dragon didn't put any herbs on her cooking, but still her dragon flames imbued the meat with a smokiness that I'd become quite partial to.

Obviously, there was no way I could eat a whole cow, but with Salanraja there I wouldn't have to. Though, I did hope that she would leave some leftovers.

The roast carcass spanned the unexposed corner of Salanraja's chamber, where I had once sprayed and never would do so again, given I'd almost got scorched in the process. Next to this was a wide opening that looked out over the open world. Out there, a murder of crows had gathered in the distance, flying in a loose formation around and around. It was as if they were waiting for something to happen. But they didn't seem to dare come anywhere near Dragons-bond Academy.

Crows were weird – I'd always thought that. Mind you, they were one of the birds that no cat back home wanted to pick a fight with – vicious things that they were. I turned back to Salanraja, who was munching on a massive chunk of beef that she'd torn off the ribcage. I also had a pile of beef that I'd chewed off into chunks. I took hold of one in my mouth and munched.

"*Have you heard about a new Driar here in Dragonsbond Academy?*" I asked Salanraja in my mind.

"*No one told me that the Driars were recruiting.*"

"*Well, I saw someone. A woman just now. She looked a little odd.*"

Salanraja chuckled. "*She's probably one of the guards. Or a student you've not noticed yet.*"

"*No. She was far too old to be a student, and she wasn't wearing armour.*"

"*Then you were hallucinating, Bengie. Maybe the hunger was getting to you.*"

I growled, and I bit into another piece of beef. Then I turned towards the crystal placed by the opening from Salanraja's chamber to the outside world. It displayed a vision of that hideous beast I'd seen in my dreams.

I really didn't want to have to face off against that thing. It would eat me. Forget about destiny and all that. It was fierce, and it had three heads for fighting with, while I only had one. Salanraja could have beaten it perhaps, but she was adamant that it was me that had to fight it.

"*You don't have a choice, you know,*" she said. "*When your crystal chooses for you to do something, you have to do it.*"

"*But we're in lockdown. The Council said no one can enter or leave.*"

"*That's where you're wrong. Any requests from a crystal take precedence over orders even from King Garmin himself. We'll go after we finish our feast.*"

"*And where exactly are we going to find a chimera?*" I asked.

"*Trust me, I know of a place.*"

Suddenly, I didn't feel so hungry. Or rather, I wanted to delay eating it all for as long as I could. This was ridiculous. I shouldn't have to go and fight something I wouldn't stand a chance against. I mean, had Salanraja seen the size of that beast? It was even larger than Astravar's demon Maine Coon.

I glanced towards the entrance to the chamber, but Salanraja had strategically placed herself in front of the archway, blocking it off. The only other way out of here was out from the side of the tower. But we were so high up that if I jumped, even if I'd land on my feet, I'd break all of my bones doing so. If only there was a bed or something I could hide under. Though, knowing Salanraja, she'd probably then set the bed on fire to force me out.

"Is that why you invited me here?" I asked.

"Say again..."

"You invited me to a delicious feast so that you could trap me here so I wouldn't have a chance but to fly with you on your stupid mission."

"It's not my mission," Salanraja said. *"As always, Bengie, you seem to fail to understand how important this is."*

"What, to walk straight up to death's door, also known as the jaws or fangs of a chimera?"

"You won't kill yourself..."

"How do you know?"

Salanraja stood up and edged towards me. She moved her head so close that I could smell the fumes from her dragonfire seeping out of her nostrils. *"Because the crystal can predict the future,"* she said, *"and it would never set a mission for someone that can kill them. Gracious demons, you can be impossible sometimes, Bengie."*

Salanraja moved even closer to me, revealing a gap small enough underneath her for me to squeeze through. I picked up another piece of beef in my mouth to make sure I had a fair serving of the lunch that Salanraja had invited me to. Then I squeezed underneath her belly, through her back legs, and out of the doorway. I sprinted down the spiral staircase, and across the slushy ground towards the water fountain. I hid underneath the stone there, going so deep that no one would be able to see me. No students were around now – everyone was in the dining hall eating roasted goose.

"*You can't escape me, Bengie,*" Salanraja said. "*I can still speak in your mind.*"

"I'm not going," I said.

"*Then you leave me no choice...*"

"What? What do you mean, Salanraja? What are you going to do?"

All went quiet inside my mind for a while, and I stared out at the empty bailey, not particularly wanting to come out from my hiding hole. Eventually Salanraja's voice came back in my head.

"*It is done,*" she said.

"*What is?*"

"*The Council of Three wants to see you. You are to go to their offices. Now!*"

Whiskers, the traitor! I wasn't going anywhere. Instead, I edged even further underneath the fountain, as I listened to the crows cawing in the distance, and the wind howling through the castle.

9

HOW TO SHOW AFFECTION

After several minutes of sulking underneath the fountain, I decided that the worst thing that I could do was stay in my hiding spot. This strategy would have worked in my own world – I was too far underneath for anyone to reach me. But the Driars in Dragonsbond Academy had magic that they could use to pull me out with ease.

The Council of Three had already demonstrated how they could raise me up in the air using beams of light from their staffs and pin me there, completely paralysed. I was sure that they would do a lot worse to me if I didn't heed their summons.

I walked through the open archway to the Council's Courtyard. But the Council hadn't asked to meet me here. For the first time in my life, I'd actually meet them in their own office.

I had thought that the door might present a problem. The heavy walnut-oak door to the keep was usually closed with one of those round handles that cats didn't have a chance of opening. The door had a knocker on it, but that was far out of reach.

Fortunately, the door was slightly ajar this time, and I pushed it a little further using all my strength. It wasn't easy, I tell you. Tasks which often seem simple for a human are a lot harder for a cat. But saying that, there's also an awful lot of things that cats can do that humans can't.

The door creaked open a little more, and I pushed my way around it. I entered an office – a wide and tall room with a curved standing reception desk at the centre of it. Two red-carpeted staircases flanked the room leading up to a mezzanine. Doors led off in all directions.

Each staircase had a bench underneath it, and Bellari and Rine sat on one of these, their mouths wrapped each around the other's. I have to say that I didn't get this whole kissing thing that lovers – if I could call Bellari and Rine that – did to show affection. It wasn't just gross, but also utterly pointless.

The two were so engrossed in what they were doing that they didn't seem to notice me enter the room. I thought that I could have some fun with this, and so I took a deep breath, then I bawled out in the mightiest voice I could muster, "Initiate Rine!"

Rine jumped up off the bench and spun around. "What? Who?" He looked around the room in confusion, and then he turned down and glared at me. "Ben!"

His girlfriend, Bellari, sneezed. "Rine, it's that cat again. Get him out of here."

I growled. Initiate Bellari was perhaps my worst enemy in the whole of Dragonsbond Academy, including some of the more ignorant cats who didn't seem to appreciate a Bengal, a descendent of the great Asian leopard cat I might add, marking what they considered their territory.

"You know," I said. "I don't think you're allergic to cats at all, Bellari."

"How dare you. Of course I'm allergic. I sneeze whenever I see one."

"And do you sneeze when you don't see one?"

Her face went a bright shade of puce. "I—What in the seventh dimension are you talking about?"

I moved over to her, and she backed up against the bench. Her eyes were red as if she'd been crying. She and Rine must have been making up after an argument.

"You know, I learned quite an interesting word when I gained the ability to speak your language," I said. "Psychosomatic."

"Psycho-what?"

"Oh, your civilisation will learn that word when you decide you have a need for psychology."

Bellari's nostrils flared. "Who do you think you are? And what in the Seventh Dimension are you talking about?"

I jumped up on the bench and pushed up to her, rubbing my nose against her elbow. This, you see, is the proper way to show affection, even if Bellari didn't really deserve it. She immediately shot up out of her seat and backed up against the wall. "I told you not to go anywhere near me. Rine, do something..."

I leaped off the bench, and I followed her towards the wall until I had her backed into a corner.

Rine was watching the whole encounter, and he looked as if he was trying to stop himself from laughing. "He's right, you know. Ben's an Initiate now, and you've got to start treating him like one of us."

Bellari sneezed again, and I flinched but stayed in my spot looking up at her. I let out a meow for good measure.

"I do hope you're joking," Bellari said.

"There's no need to be so cruel to him, sugarpot. He saved us from a demon dragon, remember. He's a hero."

"He's a cat. Rine, I swear, get this cat away from me, or I'll—"

"You'll do what?"

"Don't test me," Bellari said. Really, she looked so funny when her face went red like this, contrasting boldly against her rich blonde curls.

Rine sighed. "Fine." He walked over, scooped me up in his arms, and carried me to the other side of the room. I nestled myself into the warm folds of his cloak, purring deeply. I got on much better with Rine now than when I'd first met him. I admit, he still seemed a bit of a snob. But his girlfriend was much, much worse.

Bellari crossed her arms. "Make sure you change clothes and bathe before you come near me again, Rine."

Rine sighed and looked down at me, turning away from his girlfriend. "So... What brings you here, Ben? I heard you were scheduled to have lunch with your dragon."

"I've already eaten. Then the Council of Three summoned me here."

"Really?" Rine took me over to a dusty smelling open book on the desk with what looked like names scrawled on after the other on the page. "You're not on the list."

"Probably because they only just summoned me."

"Oh," Rine said. "Well, there's a meeting in there right now." He turned towards the large double doorway underneath the mezzanine.

"A meeting? About what?"

"Aren't you the nosy one," Rine said with a chuckle. "I don't know much, and I'm not allowed to tell you what I do know."

"I guess I'll wait then," I tried to pull myself out of Rine's arms and jump down towards Bellari to annoy her some more. But he held me there with a firm grip.

"Oh no," Rine said in a hushed voice. "Come on, Ben, you've already got me in enough trouble today. Don't go causing more."

"Fine," I said with a growl. But I didn't push it. Instead, I watched the double doors to the Council Room, wondering when the meeting would finally finish inside. I didn't wait long. After a few minutes, perhaps, the doors swung open and they stayed open. No one was standing by the door, so I guessed someone must have opened them through magic.

Rine dropped me down on the floor. "Go on in, it's your turn I guess."

I considered going over to annoy Bellari even more, fun as the game was. She returned a sneer at me and made a shooing motion towards the Council Room. Well, it was probably better to not keep the Council of Three waiting.

Behind the double doors to the Council Room, I could already see the three Council members sitting at their desks. I raised my head high, and I strolled into the room.

10

COUNCIL BUREAUCRACY

The three desks were arranged in the Council Room, much as the lecterns were outside. Each was made of sturdy looking hardwood, with papers and ornaments scattered all over them. The room was much warmer than outside, too – which I greatly appreciated. Heat roared out of two fireplaces stacked with burning logs on either side of the room. The air also had a much cleaner taste to it than it did in any other room in the castle, as if someone dusted here three times a day.

Driar Yila sat at the left desk, her head resting in her cupped hands as she peered at me inquisitively. Driar Lonamm was at the centre desk, shaking her head, and I wasn't sure if this was due to what had happened in her previous meeting with Prefects Lars and Asinda or because I was in a lot of trouble. Driar Brigel was gazing up at the ceiling nonchalantly. Three high arched windows stood behind each desk, with a stained-glass depiction of each of the Driar's dragons at the top of each window.

Apparently, you got summoned here when the Council of Three didn't even deem it worth their while to step outside. Their staffs were propped in racks within easy reach of them, at the sides of their desks. I was sure that if I tried anything funny, they wouldn't hesitate to punish me with their magic.

From here, I could also see there was far too much stuff on the desks, and some of it belonged on the floor. I turned my head from desk to desk, wondering which bit of paper or trinket I should knock off first.

"What are you doing, cat?" Driar Yila asked.

"I thought you knew my name now, ma'am," I said, drawing out the last word slightly to demonstrate my annoyance.

"I shall use your name while you're in our good graces. When you aren't, I shall call you what I please. Now answer my question."

"I'm merely examining your papers..."

"Why?" Driar Lonamm asked.

"They look interesting..."

"If you knock anything off the desk, I'll skin you alive," Driar Yila said, and she leaned forwards and wrapped her hand around her staff. The red crystal at the top of it glowed at her touch.

I growled, and I sank down onto my haunches. "Fine," I said. "I'll be good."

Driar Lonamm was shaking her head. "You've got a lot to learn. Now a little bird told me that you've been refusing your crystal's calling."

"By 'little bird', do you mean 'rather big dragon'?" I asked.

"I mean that my dragon told me what your dragon told him. Now, it's meant to be us that's asking the questions. What reasons have you for refusing the call?" She glared at me as she asked the question, looking no less fierce than Driar Yila.

I turned to Driar Brigel, hoping for a little sympathy. But he also had a massive frown on his face. I tried to give the Driars a wide-eyed look – a kind of magic 'cuteness' spell that always worked in my world – but none of them were having any of it.

"Initiate Ben," Driar Brigel said. "I don't think you understand the responsibility of being a dragon rider. The crystal gave you a gift not so you could do what you please, but so you could work for the future of the kingdom."

"But I have to face a beast that's bigger than me and could eat me for breakfast, dinner, or supper. There's no way I can defeat a chimera."

"That's where you're wrong," Driar Lonamm said. "The crystal wouldn't reveal to you a destiny that leads to your death."

"Unless such death could save the entire kingdom," Driar Yila added.

I swallowed hard as my heart started thumping in my chest. I just couldn't believe what I was hearing. These people, they'd grown up with these crystals and they'd based their entire belief system around them. But I didn't come from their world, and so I couldn't trust a massive gem, magical or not.

"No," I said. "I'm not doing it. I don't want to die."

I must have said that extremely loudly or something, because my words reverberated off the room's walls, decaying into silence.

"*You have some nerve,*" Salanraja said in my mind. "*Don't you think it's less scary to just go on this mission than deal with the punishments the Council of Three can enact on you?*"

"*They can do what they like,*" I said. "*Because they won't catch me.*"

I turned and sprinted towards the open doors. But I could only take a few steps before a massive gust of wind came from the doorway and a green glowing light exploded from the centre of the opening. Then the doors slammed shut in my face. I turned back to see that Driar Brigel had his staff pointed at the door, his staff's crystal glowing green.

One thing I'd learned in his classes was that the leaf magic in his crystal gave him the power to manipulate nature. That included, I guessed, the ability to telekinetically swing wooden doors on their own hinges.

"You have to learn to rise above your instincts, Ben," Driar Brigel said. "Fear always wants you to take the easy way out, but more often than not that path isn't good for you."

"My instincts? I'll have you know I consider my actions quite carefully. It's just I'm an extremely fast thinker."

"If your thoughts were that fast," Driar Lonamm said. "Then you'd have realised there was no point in running. With this entire castle on lockdown, you have nowhere to go."

Suddenly there came a banging at the door, startling me for the second time.

"Yes," Driar Yila said, and I skittered out of the way of the opening door.

Captain Onus, the head of the guards here, stood at the entrance, together with a female guard. The captain looked down at me with his ugly face, pursed his lips and made a sucking sound as if he wanted to endear himself to me.

"Yes, Captain," Driar Yila said again.

Captain Onus seemed to remember himself. He stood to attention and then gave a bow. An expression of alarm returned to his face. "It's the Cat Sidhe. I really don't know how, but she's escaped."

WHERE DID SHE GO?

We didn't waste any time leaving the Council Office. The three Driars were immediately up on their feet and storming out of the doors. There must have been a good reason why Astravar had wanted Ta'ra so badly, but no one had told me exactly why yet.

Outside, in the bailey, a thick fog had settled on the academy. Though I couldn't see them, I could hear the crows high above the castle, screeching into the air. The cats, my brothers and sisters, crouched watching where the sounds came from, waiting for a crow to emerge from the cover. Everything was cold now – the ground, the fog, the howling wind that cut through it, and the sinking feeling that Astravar had stolen Ta'ra away from us. What did he want of her? Was he using her as a trap to try to get hold of me?

I saw something falling from the sky, and I leaped out of the way of a crow-dropping that splattered on the ground. Thank goodness I still had my wits about me, because the last thing I wanted was the excrement from those ugly birds ruining my beautiful silky fur.

The Driars had ordered me to stay close to them, and after what

Driar Brigel had done to those doors, I didn't think it was a good idea to argue with them. They led me over to the gate tower where Ta'ra had been locked away. A guard was waiting outside there, his posture sunken, and I guessed he was probably the culprit. I wanted to scratch him to teach him a lesson, but every inch of his body from the neck down was covered in light armour.

"What happened here?" Driar Yila asked the guard. "I thought you had her under lock and key."

"I did," the guard replied. "We sealed off any gaps underneath the door, and I had one of the prefects make sure there was nothing on the ground she could have crawled through."

"So how could she have escaped?" Driar Brigel asked, one hand on his hip, the other on his chin. "I checked the wards Initiate Ange had set and all of them were sound."

"We have no idea," Captain Onus said. "That's what we're trying to work out."

A door creaked open behind me, and Aleam came out of it. He quickly hobbled over to us, using his staff for support. "I've just heard the news," he said, coming to a stop next to the three Council members.

Everyone turned towards Driar Aleam.

"Do you have any idea how she might have escaped?" Driar Lonamm asked him.

"No," Aleam said. "But we need to examine all possibilities. The crows are still up in the air," – he pointed at them with his staff – "and I don't think any of them would have got past our cats."

"What can a crow do?" I asked.

"You have no idea..." Aleam said, looking down at me and shaking his head. "But I think the major question right now, is what does Astravar want with Ta'ra?"

Aleam and the Council of Three continued to interrogate the guards. Meanwhile, I looked up at the crows, and I wondered if

49

Ta'ra could have been there among them. Maybe Astravar had somehow turned her into one of those foul birds. She could get shot down by an arrow, without the guards knowing who she was. Then, the cats might come in and try to eat her – even though crow tastes disgusting. But some of my brothers and sisters looked so malnourished, they probably wouldn't even care.

"Ben?" Aleam asked me.

"Huh?" I said, and I realised that I'd been daydreaming, perhaps even almost dozing off.

"Did you see anything funny around here? You were in the courtyard just moments ago, and Ta'ra must have escaped around the same time."

I didn't know. I pressed the rewind button on my life for the last hour or so, and I remembered the council being mean to me, annoying Bellari just before I caught the two kissing, Salanraja nagging me about fighting the chimera, and the delicious beef. Then what was before that? Oh, it was always so hard to remember anything before the food.

Then I remembered climbing the staircase, following that delicious aroma of smoky beef, mesmerised. Before the staircase there was that woman – the one with the raven black hair, dark coat, and the white blouse.

"I saw someone," I said. "Just before I went up to see Salanraja."

Aleam raised an eyebrow, and he leaned towards me on his staff. "Go on..."

"There was a woman. I'd never seen her before."

"What did she look like?" Driar Lonamm asked.

"Well, she had a black robe, a white shirt underneath it, and black hair. Come to think of it, her clothing looked a bit like..." I trailed off, as the implications dawned on me.

"You're kidding," Driar Brigel said.

"No," Driar Lonamm said. "Astravar can make her do that?"

"She's used one of her nine transformations," Aleam said. He examined the door. "A fairy, small enough to fit through the keyhole. Did anyone put any wards on the lock?"

Driar Brigel lowered his head. "I didn't think to tell Initiate Ange to do that... I'm sorry, Aleam."

"No time for apologies," Aleam said. "We must go out there and find her. But where might she have gone?"

That was a mighty good question. Of course, I wasn't really the best creature to ask. I'd never even heard of fairies until I entered this world and met Ta'ra for the first time, and that hadn't been so long ago.

The four older Driars had now turned towards the keep tower. That building apparently contained the most powerful of the dragons, including Olan – Aleam's white dragon.

"I'll go now." He walked off towards the keep.

"Me too," I called after him, but Driar Brigel put out a hand to stop me.

"You have a mission, young one," he said.

Whiskers, I'd hoped they'd forgotten about it. Even if searching for Ta'ra might have turned out to be more dangerous, I'd rather do that than face a chimera.

"*Bengie,*" Salanraja said in my mind. "*Has Aleam gone yet?*"

"*No,*" I replied. "*Why?*"

"*Stop him now!*"

"*Why?*"

"*Just do it.*"

Aleam had already travelled halfway across the bailey towards the Council Courtyard. I tried to shout out, but he didn't seem to hear me. So, I sprinted after him, half expecting Driar Brigel to cast a magic spell to stop me.

"Stop!" I shouted.

Driar Aleam turned around. "Ben, we haven't got time for this. You must respect your crystal's wishes."

"It's not me that's telling you to stop, it's Salanraja."

He paused a moment. "Why? What is it?"

I asked Salanraja the same question.

"*It's the crystal,*" she said. "*It's giving us a little bit more information on our mission to fight the chimera, which seems to involve Ta'ra and Astravar...*"

I groaned from deep in my stomach, because I really wasn't sure I liked the sound of that. Battling a chimera was one thing. But having to battle a chimera, Astravar, his demon Maine Coon, and whatever horrible creatures he might have summoned from the Seventh Dimension sounded a lot, lot worse.

But still, I knew we needed to discover what the crystal knew. So, I told Aleam exactly what Salanraja had said.

12

THE VISION

Inside her own chamber, Salanraja watched our crystal from the entranceway. The three dragons belonging to the Council of Three and Aleam's white dragon, Olan, hovered outside, flapping their wings every several seconds to keep them aloft.

Unusually, each of the Council had dragons that matched the colour of their staffs. Driar Yila had a ruby dragon called Farago, just like Salanraja except Farago had no spikes on his back. Driar Lonamm's dragon was a sapphire, known as Flue, with exceptionally long teeth. And Driar Brigel had an emerald dragon called Plishk that, just like the gentle giant, carried a lot of extra muscle bulk.

The three Driars and Aleam had huddled closest to the exposed opening, as if ready to mount their dragons at any moment. I had taken a place by my meal of beef, and I chewed on a piece of it for comfort, even if I didn't feel like eating. It had dried out, anyway. Knowing Salanraja, she'd probably roasted it a second time deliberately evaporating any tantalising moisture out of it to express her anger for my disagreement before.

The crystal emanated a warmth that felt like the setting sun. It was spinning slowly on its vertical axis, just by the opening. This meant that it had something important to say. Last time it did this, it had wanted to gift me my ability to speak multiple languages. But this time it didn't bring good news.

Instead, two of my fears had combined to create an even greater fear. When I'd last faced off against Astravar, I'd had to battle a massive beast he'd summoned from the Seventh Dimension. And I'm not talking about the demon dragon.

I'd gone up against a beast of nightmares, something no cat should ever have to face. I shuddered every time I thought about how Astravar's demon Maine Coon had pinned me to the ground and almost killed me.

But now, beneath the facets of the crystal, I could see Astravar riding the beast. Except, this wasn't the Maine Coon I'd last encountered – but then the old Ragamuffin in South Wales had always said that you never encounter the same cat twice. As before, it had cracks all over its body, revealing the lava boiling underneath its skin. The Maine Coon also had that same face, with its ashen lion-like mane. But it now had gained a snake for a tail and a second neck with a goat's head sticking out of it.

In other words, the demon Maine Coon was now a demon chimera, and I couldn't believe my eyes.

The snake tail of the beast was covered in flames and lashed out violently into the air as Astravar gripped the goat's horns like handles and rode it onwards. The view in the crystal zoomed out to show his companions – thousands of black cats, twice the size of panthers, with white tufts on their chests.

They had a massive crystal with them too. This was purple and hovered in the air above Astravar and his demon chimera. Thin tendrils of light emanated from this crystal, each of them connecting with a Cat Sidhe below.

Together Astravar and his companions sprinted, and the purple crystal floated, towards a massive city that stretched across the horizon. This was Cimlean, the capital city of Illumine, residence of King Garmin and what I'd heard was an opulent palace. It looked so innocent there, its marble walls lit in a brilliant, almost blinding white and the golden towers glinting in the sunlight. Around the city, the whiteness of the snow on the ground and the pine trees added to this image of pureness.

But this snow would soon dissolve, I realised, once the purple acrid mist that Astravar and his army of black cats carried around them seeped into the city and slowly choked it of life. Still, the city wasn't defenceless, and I could already see the archers standing like dominoes upon the city's walls.

"An invasion," Driar Lonamm said, "but how could Astravar get such a large army, and what is that beast he's riding?"

"I don't know," Driar Brigel replied. "He's clearly learned a new spell."

"They're Cat Sidhe," Driar Yila said. "All of them. He must have stolen them from the Faerie Realm."

"Which is why he wanted to capture Ta'ra," Aleam said. "To open a portal."

If you'd asked me a year ago, I wouldn't even have known what a magical portal was. As far as the cats in our South Wales clowder knew, there was only one world, with oceans and deserts and great plains like the Savannah, and the jungles from where my powerful ancestors, the great Asian leopard cats, came. More recently, I'd learned from my lessons with Driar Brigel that there were actually seven worlds, or dimensions, interlinked, with the seventh being the scariest of all. That was where the demons lived.

The first was this one, the second the Faerie Realm, the third the Ghost Realm, and the fourth the Earth I knew so well and longed to return to. The fifth and the sixth dimensions were more mysterious, as no magician – not even Astravar – had learned to open them yet, and so no one knew what lived within them.

"Still, we've not yet completely answered my question," Driar Lonamm said. "How did Astravar obtain such powerful magic? We're talking about alteration powerful enough to convert an entire fairy city population to his cause. What channel could he possibly be using?"

Everyone turned to Aleam. He was the oldest, and the only one here who knew dark magic as well as the warlocks. If it weren't for his dragon, Aleam would have also been corrupted by dark magic. But Olan saved him, so the legend goes, from his darkest hour.

"It's that crystal," Aleam said. "In all my time when I was dark mage for the king, we never even imagined a dark crystal that large. It has a lot of power in it, and I'm guessing Astravar plans to use it to capture the fairies' souls. Somehow, though, Ta'ra must be the key."

"The key to what?" Driar Yila asked.

"Perhaps he's using her love to channel the power..." Driar Brigel said as he gazed out towards the horizon. "Didn't you say, Aleam, that Ta'ra was betrothed to a prince before Astravar turned her into a cat?"

Aleam nodded. "She was cast out of that society long ago. Branded by the fairies as a fae because she had dark magic nestled within her. After Astravar summoned her from her wedding ceremony, she tried to return. But once Prince Ta'lon, her betrothed, realised what she'd become, he cut off all ties with her. From what I've heard about that prince, I'm not sure he ever loved Ta'ra in the first place. Although admittedly I've only heard the story from one source."

Driar Brigel nodded. "I guess she still loved him. And we all know from the fairy tales that unrequited love can spawn the worst type of magic."

Aleam sighed but said nothing.

I remembered the crystal that I'd swallowed back when Salanraja and I had battled the golem. It still was lodged within me, apparently, now nestled within the creases of my brain. In all honesty, it wasn't because I was a cat but rather because of the existence of that dark magic within me that made so many students here wary of me. So, I kind of understood how Ta'ra must have felt.

Inside the display on my crystal, Astravar and his army had now reached the city, and the archers fired their first volley. As the army moved, the purple mist around them seemed to seep into the land, melting the snow and sending up smoky steam. Arrows fell all around the warlock who had his staff raised up in the air, glowing purple at its tip. He cast a spell that created a bubble around him. Some arrows hit this but bounced off. Others hit the sides of the cats, some of which collapsed on the battlefield.

Presently, Astravar reached down into his pouch and lifted out a handful of small crystals. He threw these in the direction of the city, and they followed his trajectory for a moment, before lighting up in blue and then following a much straighter path of their own. As they shot forwards, they split up into more and more trails of light, creating a display that looked like those scary fireworks that humans liked to let off back home.

The view, kindly, followed the path of one of these crystals so we could see their effects up close. They continued in a straight line, not even seeming to waver, until they found their way right into the archers' heads. But the magic didn't kill them. Rather, the archers' eyes filled with white, and a blue spot glowed at the top of their head. Soon, they turned their bows away from the ground towards the sky. The view panned upwards and around to show dragons soaring in from the distance.

There must have been hundreds of them flying in from Dragonsbond Academy. The archers loosed their arrows at the dragons. In flight, these arrows took on a purple hue, sending out a trail of that magical gas behind them. Many of them hit the riders and knocked them off their mounts. Others buried themselves into the dragons' flanks and wings.

Despite the onslaught, still some dragons broke through and unleashed fire upon Astravar, who had a massive blue energy shield all around him to ward off the flames.

The view panned around to show a wide angle across the battlefield, the dragons now flying away from Astravar and starting to regroup. Suddenly, the air around these dragons began to twinkle, and then it filled with a flowing yellow powder. On the ground, the number of Cat Sidhe had reduced to around half.

"As I thought," Aleam said. "Astravar has the fairies completely under his control. He must be using the ones he's sent into the sky as conduits for his dark magic."

I didn't want to watch the rest of the scene, but my eyes seemed glued to what was happening, and I couldn't turn my head away. Everywhere around the dragons, explosions blossomed – brilliant displays of fire and light. I couldn't hear anything that was happening in the crystal, as it didn't seem quite as sophisticated as television back home. But still I could feel the dragons' anguish as they tossed their heads to the sky and gnashed and roared before they came crashing down to the ground.

The battlefield was presently reduced to ash, rubble, and smoke, with that horrible purple mist surrounding Astravar and his demon chimera Maine Coon, who were both protected by their shield barrier. Soon, the glistening wisps in the air came back down to ground. But they didn't transform back into the Cat Sidhe. Rather, they settled there on the ground, as if their life force had been extinguished.

"He's going to kill them," Driar Yila said. "He's sacrificed those fairies' lives to kill our own dragons."

"Ta'ra," I muttered, then, my breath caught in my throat before

I could say anything else. Ta'ra could have been one of those fairies. He would just send her out to sacrifice her. Is that all her life, or all any of these fairies' lives meant to Astravar? A weapon to take down his enemies.

Astravar pulled back his magical bubble-shield, and then he pointed at the city walls with his staff. Together, the remaining Cat Sidhe and the warlock charged at the city, with nothing to protect it. The archers on the walls also turned their arrows upon the city and rained down volleys of fiery arrows upon their own kind.

Soon Cimlean went up in flames. The light from the fires became an intense white light glowing out from the crystal, which then spoke inside my head.

"*This is the fate that will become of this world,*" it said. "*If you fail to face up to your destiny, Initiate Ben. Soon after, Astravar will take his battle across all worlds, and everything shall be destroyed.*"

Every single muscle in my body was trembling, and I needed to sit down. I don't know what I feared more – the demon chimera, Astravar destroying all sources of food across the dimensions, or what he might do to Ta'ra.

I couldn't let it happen. I couldn't let Astravar take control. But I hated it. Part of me just wanted to go home back to my normal world where I didn't have to worry about anything.

Growling, I turned back to the four Driars whose faces were so white that they looked like they'd just seen a thousand ghosts.

13

AN UNLIKELY VOLUNTEER

The crystal had now dimmed to a dull grey, displaying nothing more. The entire scene had sent the four Driars into agitation, and they were currently discussing how to react.

"The portal Ta'ra came through to get to his world is in the Willowed Woods," Aleam said. "And so, I'm guessing that's where Ta'ra is heading now."

Driar Yila bristled, and her face blanched. "We sent Prefect Asinda and High Prefect Lars out there yesterday. We heard there was an anomaly in the area, and we needed someone to investigate. Now, it sounds we may have sent my niece and her boyfriend into grave danger."

I often forgot that Prefect Asinda was Driar Yila's niece, which might have explained why the younger woman acted so angry around me all the time – because, simply put, that anger ran in the family.

Aleam shook his head. "We'll find a way to help them. But we must go out there at once."

"But who should we send?" Driar Brigel asked.

"I'll go," I said.

That sent the room into silence. The Council of Three looked down at me, each of them with surprised looks on their faces. From the corner of the room, Salanraja let out a croon which sounded almost like a mewl.

"*You've changed your tune,*" she said to me. "*What happened to being scared of the chimera?*"

An image flashed into my mind of the demon chimera that Astravar had managed to acquire, one head roaring, another bleating, and the third lashing out towards me with a venomous hiss. I hadn't a clue how I was meant to fight that thing. It had almost slaughtered me without effort the last time I'd encountered it, and that was before it had grown two extra heads. "*I'm not letting that evil warlock destroy all the fish and mutton and venison and delicious things in this world,*" I said. "*What will there be left to eat then?*"

Salanraja chuckled in my mind. "*Are you sure it's nothing to do with Ta'ra?*"

"*What are you talking about? She's a fairy and I'm a cat.*"

"*But she won't be if she changes into a fairy one more time. She'll then become a cat forever.*"

"*Salanraja, this is nonsense.*"

"*We will see... We will see,*" Salanraja said, and she chuckled in my mind once again.

While Salanraja spoke in my mind, the three members of the Council were studying me. Probably, they also wanted some time to talk to the dragons about my sudden decision. I could imagine that they were trying to work out what to do if I took the first opportunity I had to run away from this lockdown. But I wasn't going to run away. I didn't want to risk being eaten by spiders and serkets again.

Aleam also watched me, but his expression was so passive, I

didn't know what he was thinking. Eventually, it was Driar Yila who spoke.

"It makes sense to send the cat, I think," she said, though since she'd first mentioned Asinda her face hadn't regained its colour. "There's no better creature to track the Cat Sidhe across the land. You'll know her scent, I guess?"

"I'm not like a dog," I said. "I don't hunt creatures down for sport."

Driar Yila frowned. "But when push comes to shove, you'll be able to track her." Her voice was flatter than usual.

"Of course I can. Cats can smell better than dogs. In fact, we have one of the best senses of smell of any creature alive." I didn't know, in all honesty, if the last sentence was true. But I thought it sounded good enough to say. Then I added for good measure, "Oh, and because I'm a descendant of the great Asian leopard cat, that makes my olfactory sensibilities even greater than your typical moggie."

"Good," Driar Lonamm said, "But we're going to need to put a team together. This isn't just about stopping Ta'ra but also about sending reinforcements to help Prefect Lars and Prefect Asinda."

"I agree," Driar Brigel said. "This isn't a task for Initiates or Prefects anymore. We must send some of our Driars out there, even if it means putting classes on hold."

"Surely, none of you three are thinking of going out there?" Aleam said.

"Oh no," Driar Yila said, shaking her head. "Though I feel I should help my family, it's probably unwise for me to go out and face Astravar at my age. I'm sure Driar Lonamm and Driar Brigel feel the same." She looked at each of them and they each returned a nod.

"I understand," Aleam said. "But you probably realise that I will have to go."

"I thought you'd say that," Driar Brigel replied. "And we also need to send Seramina. After what happened with Ta'ra, we need to look after Initiate Ben's dreams."

I was already regretting my decision to go. There are some people that cats just don't like, and that weird blonde-haired teenager was one of them. I looked out at the dragons hovering outside. They were watching our conversation with intent, and I had no doubt that the Council of Three was also asking them for ideas.

Then I wondered. Maybe I could take another of those dragons, rather than Salanraja. They might be a little gentler with me in flight after being so experienced carrying old people across the land.

"*I heard that,*" Salanraja said.

"*Well, don't you feel you need a holiday?*"

But Salanraja didn't have time to answer before the crystal cut into our conversation. Suddenly, it glowed white, though this time it didn't display any mysterious scenes. And, instead of speaking in my head, it pulsed out light to the rhythm of its words. It was strange – I'd never heard it speak out loud before.

It still had that beautiful Welsh sounding voice though. I had no idea why this crystal liked to speak just like the humans back home. I wondered if there was a human in a room back in my world some-where controlling it all.

"The cat must choose the team," the crystal said.

Driar Brigel was the first to spin around and stare at the crystal in surprise. Then, the other two members of the Council cast their gaze upon it. Aleam was the last to turn around. No one said anything – they had great deference for the crystal, almost as if they saw it as some kind of religious deity.

"This will be another test," the crystal continued. "Initiate Ben will one day lead armies into battle, and so he must learn to make such decisions for himself."

Driar Yila grimaced at these words, Driar Lonamm frowned, and Driar Brigel crossed his arms. I started purring and rubbed myself against the crystal. It did, after all, have that pleasant warmth to it that combated the icy breeze coming from the exposed opening. I just wished its predictions didn't involve getting me into danger all the time.

Soon, the warmth died down from the crystal, and the light faded once again. Salanraja was glaring at me from the corner of the room, clearly insulted that I'd considered riding another dragon. I don't know why she took these things so personally.

"Because I'm bonded to you," Salanraja said to me. *"And flying another dragon is worse than adultery in a relationship. Unless, doing so might save your life, that is."*

"Well, flying a more able dragon might decrease my chances of getting thrown off from miles high."

"And what's that meant to mean?"

"Nothing...Fine, you can come. I wasn't ever going to not take you. But I need to work out the rest of the team. It sounds like quite a task the crystal has set for me."

"Then tell the Council that. Show them you can act responsibly, because right now the Council of Three and their dragons think we're all doomed."

I opened my mouth to say just that. But before a single word came out, Driar Yila raised her hand. "Don't say anything. Just gather your team, and then we'll meet you down at the Council Courtyard to brief you on your mission."

I glanced at Aleam, who shrugged. Then, I slinked off down the stairway, and I went to search out my team.

14

BELLARI OR ANGE?

I went first to the fountain, and there I found Rine once again kissing Bellari. The students were on their break and they laughed and danced and played that strange game with the string and the hourglass-shaped wood.

It had warmed now, with the sun shining down from the sky. This melted the snow off the parapets, which drip-drip-dripped onto the stone below. From the kitchens came the aroma of smoked trout. It seemed a shame that we'd have to fly away and miss this meal, although maybe I'd be able to convince Matron Canda to pack some of it for our journey so we could eat it for supper.

Rine and Bellari seemed oblivious to everything going on around them. Which was a shame, because I'd hoped that I'd caused a bit of tension between them before, as I really wanted to push Rine towards Ange. I'd said it before, and I'll say it again – she was a far better mate for Rine. Ange wouldn't only teach him a lot about magic, but also about how to care for cats.

Maybe, if I didn't find my way back to my own world, I could one day convince Rine and Ange to settle down in a pleasant cottage somewhere, away from scary things like wolves and serkets and demon chimeras. Then they could feed me nice food, perhaps hunted and cooked by Salanraja.

Ta'ra could be there too once we rescued her. She only had one more transformation left, after all, before she became a cat forever. I could look after her, and teach her how to roam the village, how to hunt for sport, and how to mark and guard territory.

But, as tempting as it was to do so, I didn't have time for daydreaming right now. I only had an hour to recruit my team, and I already knew that Rine and I fought well together. He'd helped me bring down the demon dragon, and though his ice bolts had done little against it, I was still sure he'd be able to help in a pinch.

The first thing I had to do was put a stop to their pointless displays of affection, and there was no better way to do so than jump up on the fountain and rub myself up against Bellari's back.

"What?" Bellari said, spinning around. As soon as she saw me, she leapt up off her perch. She turned away from me to sneeze, and then she backed up. "I thought I told you to stay away from us. Why do you keep ruining our private time, you stupid cat?"

I looked around at all the teenagers talking and playing in the bailey. "It's hardly private."

"That's because we're banned from doing such things in the corridors. Rine, remember what we talked about? Get him away!"

Her screaming was damaging my sensitive eardrums, and so I flattened my ears against my head. I looked up at Rine, purring, and mewled for some affection. He sighed, shaking his head.

"Ben, Bellari wanted to kindly request that you don't come near her. She really doesn't react well to you. It's nothing personal, but these are medical reasons. You should respect that."

I growled. "I didn't come to annoy her. I came because you've been requested on a mission."

Rine raised an eyebrow. "By who?"

"By me. My crystal deemed that I was to pick a team to go out and find Ta'ra and also rescue Prefect Asinda and Prefect Lars."

"I don't think those two need rescuing," Rine replied with a chuckle. Then he looked at me incredulously. "Wait, you're serious, aren't you?"

"I need to pick a team of four dragon riders and four dragons. We're to meet in the Council Courtyard before the next strike of the clock. It's very important, Rine. If we don't act soon, all the food in every single dimension could get destroyed."

I looked over at Bellari, who had placed her hands on her hips. "If you're going out into danger again, Rine, I'm coming with you."

"But your allergies might get in the way," I pointed out.

"I won't go anywhere near you on my dragon," Bellari said. "Besides, you might need a good fire mage." She put her hand on the staff affixed to her back.

"It's me who chooses the team, not you," I said. "And the way you've treated me lately, I see no reason to choose you."

"I'm allergic to you, you stupid cat. What am I meant to do?"

"See, that's what I mean." I tucked my head into my neck. "You could try being a bit nicer about things."

Her face went red, and she opened her mouth, clearly ready to scream out more insults. But a voice calling out interrupted her.

"Ben," Ange said as she skipped across the bailey. "I've been looking everywhere for you."

"What does she want?" Bellari asked as she folded her arms. When I'd first met these two, they'd been good friends. But I guess now Rine's spoilt girlfriend saw Ange as a bit of a threat.

I leaped down off the fountain, and I went over and rubbed myself against Ange's foreleg, purring. She smiled and then tickled me underneath the chin.

"I hear you're going out on an important mission," Ange said.

"Well, doesn't news travel fast? Do you want to come?"

"That's why I'm looking for you, silly. In fact, Driar Brigel just told me about it and he recommended I should pop along, if possible. He said it would be good for my studies to understand some fairy magic. Particularly given I'm a leaf magic user."

Leaf magic was the reason that both Brigel's and Ange's staff were green. They had the ability to manipulate nature. Although, according to Brigel's classes, it wasn't really manipulation, but rather nature made the choice to help the magic user out. Apparently, only those who were kind of heart could use leaf magic. Nature just didn't trust everyone, in much the same way as I didn't trust Bellari.

I meowed to Ange, and she reached down, and picked me up, and carried me over to the fountain. Rine edged a little away from Ange, nervously, as Bellari scowled at her. He looked as if he wanted to stand up and move back to Bellari. But he seemed unsure if this was the best move.

"So that's it," Bellari said. "Ben, you have your team. Me, Rine, and Ange, and maybe Driar Aleam can come too, or one of the prefects."

Ange looked down at me, and gave a curious frown, as if expecting me to say something.

"I'm sorry, Initiate Bellari," I said. "But there's only room for two, and Ange would make a much better asset to the team than you will."

It wasn't just about going after Astravar, but though Ange's leaf magic might come in useful, I already had dragons to breathe fire and cook our food for us. Plus, I really didn't want Bellari there. Rine and Ange were suited for each other, and this was a perfect opportunity to finagle them together. I'd reserved the other two places for Aleam and one of the prefects. I wanted someone who was an accomplished swordsman, because I'd need all the strength possible to take down that demon Maine Coon chimera.

"I know what this is about, Ange," Bellari said. "You're trying to get between me and Rine, aren't you? I told you to stay away from him."

Ange looked at Rine, and it was his turn to look embarrassed.

"I..." he said.

But Ange would not stand for this aggression from Rine's girl-friend. She stood up, dropping me by the fountain. I went over to sit on Rine's lap.

"I've told you, Bellari. Really, there's nothing between me and Rine. I'm too busy for that kind of stuff. I've got my studies to worry about, and you know why I need to get those good grades." This, honestly, didn't sound good. I had assumed that I only needed to work on Rine to get him to realise who was better for him. But now, I clearly had to work on Ange too.

Bellari huffed. "You can't fool me. Rine, I refuse to let you go on this mission. Not without me, anyway."

"I don't think he has any choice," I said. "The crystal told me to choose, and that's what I'm doing. If he refuses, the Council will punish him severely."

Bellari was breathing heavily through her flared nostrils. She glared at me a while, then she turned her gaze on Rine. "Rine, say something. You can't let this happen. You need me there, Rine." Her breath was catching in her throat as if she was about to cry.

Rine shook his head. "You need to go and cool down, sugarpot. We'll talk when we're back, okay?"

But she didn't seem to want to hear this, because she was already storming across the bailey, and I could swear she almost tripped over a clump of snow.

"She'll get over it," Rine said with a shrug.

I walked away, satisfied that I'd made the first move in bringing Ange and Rine together. Before I went far, I looked over my shoulder and said, "Remember, be in the Council Courtyard before the clock strikes the hour."

Ange smiled and gave me a mock salute. But I'm not sure Rine even heard me, as he was watching Bellari hurrying away.

15

AN OBVIOUS CHOICE

B efore I'd learned to speak the human language, the concept of
time hadn't concerned me. Back then, it wasn't measured by a
clock, but specific moments like when my former mistress in South
Wales scooped food into my bowl, put me out of the door to go for
a run, and called me back in again. If I was late for any of those
things, it was their problem, not mine.

When I gained the ability to speak the human language, I also
learned certain human sayings. There was one that particularly
intrigued me: 'time waits for no man'. Honestly though, if we cats
had a concept of time like humans did, I'm sure we would say something like: 'cat waits for no time'.

So, deadlines like this one seemed a little unnatural to me. Time
also seemed to move faster than it should when I was on a mission,
and by the time I reached Aleam's abode, I'd already wasted twenty
minutes.

Aleam's door was ajar, and so I squeezed my way inside and
found the old man to be doing what he always seemed to do nowa-
days – working on Ta'ra's cure. A yellow solution bubbled away

inside his alembic apparatus. The soft sunlight streamed through the window, reflecting off the surface of the glass and suffusing it in an almost mystical light. Or maybe the solution was also glowing slightly. I wasn't so sure.

I meowed to let Aleam know that I'd entered the room, but he didn't quite seem to hear me. So, I took the next best measure for getting attention – I jumped right up on the desk in front of him. Aleam pushed me away.

"Ben, how many times have I told you not to jump up here? I don't want you damaging Ta'ra's cure."

"But I'm a cat and I won't knock anything off the desk that I don't want to." Admittedly, though, I quite fancied smashing this whole apparatus to pieces. I would have done, perhaps, if I didn't fear the repercussions. Aleam seemed quite gentle on the surface, but I'd seen him cast magic and I didn't doubt his wrath would be just as dangerous as that of any member of the Council of Three.

I jumped back on to the floor, growling. I didn't want Aleam to give Ta'ra the cure. I wanted her to be a cat forever, so I'd have a companion here who understood what it was to exist between worlds, a concept that no other creature knew.

"You know," Aleam said, studying me, "this time I think I've finally found the right ingredients. Really, I don't believe anything is irreversible. In the end, I guess time will always revert things back to their original state."

Now he was getting philosophical, and I knew exactly what he was getting at. Life crumbling to ash and returning to the soil and feeding the plants and all that stuff, creating a circle. It wasn't just humans who wondered what happened to us after death.

It didn't matter anyway, because once I'd fulfilled my destiny, I was going to cat heaven where I would get fed as much food as I wanted. I didn't have a clue what this food would be like, I just knew that it would be better than anything I'd tasted before.

"I don't think Ta'ra should take the cure," I said. "I think it's better that she stays a cat forever. That's what she wants."

"How can you be certain what she wants, Ben?"

"She's said so."

"Of course she says it while you're around. But when you're not there, she tells me how she misses her home and Prince Ta'lon and all her family. Those ties aren't easy to break."

I thought back to my own mother – a Bengal and descendant of the great Asian leopard cat, of course. I hadn't known her so well, really. I'd left her when I was a kitten and never actually visited her again. Family was another human concept I'd always failed to grasp. You moved on from your ancestors, and became better and more powerful versions of them, and you never looked back to the past. That was how it worked.

"She's already changed back into a fairy seven times now," I said. "If she changes back one more time, there's no going back for her, right?"

"Unfortunately, yes," Aleam said. "Which is why I want to offer her the cure as soon as we rescue her. She should have the chance to choose for herself."

Time, time, time, time, time. I realised suddenly that while we were having this conversation, I was 'wasting' it. "Well, you can offer it to her sooner," I said. "Because I also want you on this mission."

"I thought you'd say that. Who else did you choose?"

"Initiate Rine and Initiate Ange. And I told Initiate Bellari that she's not welcome."

"I'm sure she would have loved that."

"Not really. Now after you, I only need to find the strongest prefect who's agile and good with a sword. If another cat could ride a dragon, I'd choose them for sure."

Aleam frowned. "Ben, I think you're forgetting something."

"No, I'm not."

"Yes, you are. Your dreams, Ben. Astravar can control them. The Council of Three wanted to send Seramina with you for a good reason. She can stop the warlock reaching into your mind. Because it's reached the point that not even Salanraja can keep him out."

I didn't like the sound of that at all, and the noise I made from the base of my stomach expressed this. There was something about that young woman that I just didn't trust. There was this aura bristling around her that made me want to stay away from her. Then, there was the way that she stared at me with those terribly fiery eyes. Part of me wondered if she was from the Seventh Dimension, like the demon dragon and demon chimera.

"I know you don't like it, Ben," Aleam said. "But don't forget the crystal is testing you. It wants to see that you can make the right decisions so it will help you in the future."

"But I'm afraid of her."

Aleam laughed. "Of a thirteen-year-old girl?"

"Yes. It's the way she looks at me. She just seems evil. Plus, you've got to remember, she may be slight by your standards. But she's still much, much bigger than me."

"We can't understand everyone, Ben, much like many students here don't understand you. But that doesn't mean she's a bad person."

I growled again, and then I moved back towards the door. Before I left, I turned my head over my shoulder to say one more thing to Aleam.

"I'll consider your opinion," I said to placate the old man, even if I had given that opinion all the consideration it needed. "Now, don't forget to be at the Council Courtyard before the clock strikes the hour."

"I won't," Aleam said. "Just let me get this cure together and I'll be right over."

Presently, I squeezed out of the door. The next task was to find the strongest prefect for the task. Someone, I hoped, with a very pointy sword and the ability to use it. Someone who could fell a demon chimera, with one mighty swoop.

He would have to be strong, and muscular, and an excellent hunter, and probably also a decent cook. I knew the perfect young man for the task.

16

THE PREFECT OR THE WITCH?

Fate had it that the bell went off as soon as I left Aleam's study. The students went from chatting and laughing and playing games outside, to scrambling over each other in a mad-dash panic to get to the next class. I scanned the bailey for the red robes that denoted students as prefects. All of them were all heading in one direction – towards the training field in the far corner of the bailey.

I navigated through the tangle of legs and rushing students. I had to be careful in this place; everyone's eyes were always on the destination and never on the floor. Fortunately, as a Bengal and descendant of the great Asian leopard cat, I was faster than them, and so they never tripped over me – which probably would have hurt me more than it would hurt them.

It wasn't long until the stampede had passed. Given I had an all-important mission, I didn't have to worry about going to class, so I decided instead to watch from a distance, until I found who I was looking for.

The prefects had gathered around a sandy training ring that had been dug out of the snow. They chatted amongst themselves, making a racket and hurting my poor feline eardrums.

After a while, a wiry-looking man with a long salt and pepper beard and scraggly hair, whom I knew as Driar Gallant, the castle's quartermaster, stepped to the centre of the ring and shouted out at a volume that belied his slight frame. He called two students forward. One of them was a massive, heavily muscled prefect, almost as large as Driar Brigel. The other was a young man with a lithe body, cropped hair and a pockmarked face.

It was the second young man I'd been looking for – Prefect Calin, who I believed was High Prefect Lars' best friend.

Driar Gallant walked up to a weapons rack, and took from it two wooden swords, which he handed to the prefects. The giant's sword was twice the size of Prefect Calin's, which he wielded with two hands and a lumbering posture. Calin had more of a one-handed sword, which he held out in front of him in a sideways stance, with his other arm crossed along his chest, as if he was holding an imaginary shield.

The quartermaster stepped out of the ring, then he blew into a whistle that dangled from his neck. The prefects around the ring fell silent, and the giant charged forward, sending out a whiff of testosterone behind him. He roared as he went, red fury flashing in his face, and for a moment it looked like he'd flatten Calin with his attack. But the giant put too much weight into it to keep control, and Calin nimbly pivoted out of the way and put his foot out as his opponent rushed by. He waited until the giant went crashing to the floor, and then he brought his sword around towards his back.

It looked so fast that I thought Calin might break the giant's spine. But at the last moment, he slowed the sword, so it only tapped the massive student's back. It caused the giant to flinch a little, but I was sure this was because of the pain of being defeated so quickly than anything physical.

"He's quite an accomplished fighter, isn't he?" The voice came from right beside me, causing me to bristle and scarper away. When I was far enough, I turned to see that same scary teenager, the one they called Seramina. Her eyes again had that raging fire behind them as she stared at me, her face expressionless. "Although, I've heard during sparring, he's no match for High Prefect Lars. Only Prefect Asinda is rumoured to have ever beaten Lars."

I realised then what unnerved me so much about her. Every single human I'd known had a smell to them. Astravar smelled of rotten vegetable juice, these prefects in the ring smelled of human sweat, Ange smelled of catnip, and Rine smelled of whatever cologne he'd put on as a special of the day.

But Seramina had absolutely nothing I could detect on her. That wasn't normal at all.

"What are you doing here?" I asked. "Shouldn't you be in class?"

"I go where destiny takes me. It seems to have led me here. Fate told me I had to come to this spot, where you will choose me for an important mission. Thus, I am here."

I blinked off my disbelief. Something really was odd about this woman. She can't have possibly known that I was here, could she?

"I will take Initiate Rine, Initiate Ange, Driar Aleam, and now I only need to gather Prefect Calin and I have my team," I said. "I've made my decision and not you, nor destiny, nor fate, nor whatever fancy word you use to describe utter nonsense, can change that."

Her lips didn't move, but still in her tone of voice I could detect the slightest sliver of a grin. "Do leaders truly make decisions? Or do the right choices choose them?"

I really didn't want to be having this conversation with her right now. I turned away from her, back towards the ring where Driar Gallant shouted out an order once again. Prefect Calin stayed in the ring to face a young woman with dark skin, curly black hair, and high cheekbones. She looked at Calin with wide eyes, and I could smell fear upon her. Driar Gallant handed her a training sword from the weapons rack – this time the same size as Prefect Calin's. She assumed much the same stance as Calin, with her legs placed slightly wider apart.

Part of me didn't want to break up the games here, even if the clock tower said I only had twenty minutes left on the clock. So, I decided to let them have one more round, and I waited for Driar Gallant to blow his whistle.

Neither prefect charged this time. Instead, they circled each other in a kind of slow dance, with hard gazes locked on each other. They touched swords a few times, but they were merely simple parries, each move designed to test the other's mettle. This woman, whoever she was, clearly was a better fighter than the giant before. But still, she didn't look or smell like she believed she could take him down.

Eventually, Calin lunged forwards, and the female prefect pirouetted out of the way. But Calin had already predicted her move and brought his sword around in a low and narrow circle. He touched the flat of his blade to her bare kneecaps, and the female prefect puffed out her cheeks and let out a forced breath through her puckered lips. Driar Gallant blew the whistle again. He then clapped his hands, and Driar Calin left the ring, to be surrounded by a good half-dozen cheering prefects.

"How will you wake up from your dreams?" Seramina asked me. "Who will protect you from Astravar when not even your dragon can anymore?"

I growled at her to tell her I wasn't even going to entertain that thought. I stalked casually over to the prefects who had gathered around Prefect Calin and I shouted out as loudly as I could.

"Excuse me, prefects," I said, pushing through their legs. "Excuse me…"

They parted slightly, and I spun around to apprehend their expressions of wide-eyed surprise for a moment, before I turned to the man I'd been looking for. "Prefect Calin, I wish to request your presence for a mission of utmost importance. Your friends Prefect Asinda and High Prefect Lars, and also the Cat Sidhe, Ta'ra, are in grave danger. We must go out to rescue them at once."

I heard the prefect's breath catch in his throat. "That's terrible," he said. "I wish I could go, but—"

"You will do this," I interrupted, and I didn't care if he was a prefect and could order me to spend my next break in a classroom copying out the school rules. It's not as if I had hands to write with anyway, and I couldn't even read anything to copy it out. "My crystal has ordered me to choose a team, and you seem to be the strongest fighter of them all. I need you to defeat a demon chimera."

I expected Prefect Calin to be a little taken aback by my direct-ness. But instead the features sank on his face and his gaze became distant. "You don't understand... My dragon, Galludo, has been injured for a long time. She can't fly far, and so instead we defend the academy when any threats arise nearby."

The teenager, Seramina, floated over our way as Calin talked. She looked down at me with those freaky fiery eyes. Strangely, no one around here seemed scared of her. It was almost as if they didn't acknowledge her existence, making me wonder if she was really there, or just a figment of my imagination. She did have the power to control dreams. Could she perhaps also enter my mind when I wasn't dreaming?

Or maybe I was actually dreaming, and I would wake up to Ta'ra's fishy breath, snuggled up next to her. I'd discover that she hadn't really run away, and Aleam had put down a tantalising meal of roasted duck for us, and we were going to eat to our hearts' content.

"Do leaders make decisions?" Seramina said again, interrupting my daydream. "Or do good decisions choose them?"

She was definitely annoying; I would give her that.

I looked up at the clock tower. I only had ten minutes left now, and my stomach had started to rumble. If I didn't fill up my belly, then I would go hungry while flying for a long, long time. Alas, I knew it wouldn't be wise to go face to face against a demon chimera on an empty stomach.

In desperation, I scanned the prefects, wondering if any of them might fit the bill. But I'd seen how readily Calin had defeated the two of them, and I also saw how Seramina had used her powers to wake Ta'ra from her strange dream.

"Fine," I said. "You can come. Make sure you're at the Council Courtyard when the clock strikes the hour."

"I'm already there," she said, and I only needed to blink once, and she'd vanished from view.

The prefects were looking at me oddly, probably wondering who the whiskers I'd just been talking to. I let out a low growl, then I made my way to Salanraja's chamber, knowing that I had very little time left to eat my meal before our briefing was due.

17

COUNCIL BRIEFING

I arrived at the Council Courtyard with the soft taste of beef on my tongue, my stomach now content that I had eaten a good meal. Salanraja had been sleeping in the tower, and I'd let her rest because I wanted her as alert as possible when we fought Astravar and the demon chimera.

Beneath the dais that jutted out from the keep, the grass was cold and wet underfoot from snow melt. Seramina stood on my right, and I could smell her now, which meant she was present for real this time and not just a product of my mind. She wore this kind of light perfume that reminded me of snowdrops and early spring. Driar Aleam stood next to her, leaning on his staff, which he used as a walking stick as he moved around.

Rine and Ange stood on my left, an awkward distance apart from each other, even for friends. I looked over my shoulder at least once, expecting Bellari to be standing at the archway glaring at them. She wasn't. But still, I'd driven a solid thorn into their relationship, and this was going to take a while for Rine to undo.

In fact, I wasn't even sure he could undo this one. I felt that I'd done enough to push Rine into Ange's arms, and I was proud of my accomplishment. I felt proud of all of my accomplishments, really. I'd also almost picked the perfect team, with Seramina being the only part that didn't quite work in it. But at least now she smelled of something normal and sweet and not just emptiness. Everyone should have a smell, just as everyone should have a shadow.

The double doors opened to the keep behind the dais, and the Council of Three emerged. Driar Brigel came out first and took his position at the lectern on the right, which he rested his arms against while leaning forwards. Driar Lonamm came next, waddling like a penguin over to her position. She adjusted the blue-gemmed staff on her back and glanced over her shoulder at the crystal on the ceiling. Driar Yila came out last, scanning the ground in front of her like an owl as she moved forwards. She cast her gaze first on Aleam, then on Seramina. Her gaze then passed right over me before she saw Ange and Rine and shook her head.

"This is the team, you picked, Initiate Ben?" she said. "I thought you would have had at least one prefect..."

I growled back at her. "I tried, ma'am. But Seramina here convinced me out of it."

She spun around to face Seramina and stared at her for a moment. Seramina returned an incredibly passive gaze, her eyes looking almost glazed. Still, she didn't show any emotion, and she didn't seem at all scared of the most terrifying Driar in the whole of Dragonsbond Academy.

"Is this true?" Driar Yila asked her.

Seramina spoke without even moving her head. "This is the optimal team, ma'am."

Yila frowned, and then turned back to look at Driar Lonamm, who nodded at her. She looked at Driar Brigel, who also smiled.

"Very well," Driar Yila said, "then I guess we should begin the briefing."

She reached out behind her back and produced her staff. I flinched, thinking she might want to cast some magic at me. I'd learned not to trust her with her magical staff since she'd used it once to pin me up in the air and paralyse me. Fortunately, this time, she didn't seem to want to do this.

Instead, she pointed her staff at the crystal, and relief washed over me. A red beam shot out of her staff and hit the crystal at its centre, where it created a warm orange glow. Driar Lonamm then took her staff off her back and also pointed it at the crystal, creating a blue beam that melded with Driar Yila's. Shortly after, Driar Brigel also sent out a beam of green energy.

The crystal reacted to these beams, sucking up their light, glowing ever brighter. Soon enough, it had become filled with enough energy to project an image in front of it. It was just like the picture on a television. Still, there was no sound, which made it feel just a little disappointing.

My master and mistress back home had their television set up so that I could hear sounds coming from all directions at once. The master would play this trick on me sometimes, where he'd put a moving picture of lots of birds on the screen. I could hear them not just in front of me, but behind me, almost as if they had found a spot behind the sofa. It drove me nuts at first, as I scampered around the room trying to hunt down the birds which were clearly singing so close to me. That was until I realised they weren't real, but just a part of the show. After that, the joke got old pretty fast.

The image projected from the crystal displayed a wood, with trees with long droopy branches, and thin leaves projecting out of them. Willows, that's what I believe humans called them. Which is why I guess this place was called the Willowed Woods. Really, I wish humans had more imagination with certain names. I mean, when I learned the human language, I discovered there was a place in my home country called Green Park. But when is a park not green?

The canopy hung over the entire terrain, blotting out the sky, and casting deep shadows over the ground. It didn't look like a particularly friendly place, and I immediately regretted my decision to go out and rescue Ta'ra.

"The Willowed Woods," Driar Brigel said. "This is where fairies come into this land when they choose to do so, and where they leave the same way."

"It looks dark and scary," I said.

"That's because it is," Driar Yila said. "Wargs lurk within these woods, which is why the fairies chose it as their entryway. It's a land where no hunter dares tread."

Now I was getting confused. "What's a warg?"

"A creature like a wolf, but much bigger," Driar Lonamm said. "A massive lumbering beast, with red eyes and evil intent. Some say that the warlocks can control them. Others say that they just live to kill anything that crosses their path that moves."

"Which is why you mustn't camp in the Willowed Woods," Driar Brigel added. "They will hunt you for sport, and unlike wolves, they don't care if you're in a group or alone."

"And they also sometimes hunt during the day," Driar Yila added.

I didn't like the sound of any of this at all. A bitter howling wind came out of the sky and passed through my fur, causing me to shudder. "We better stay in the air then," I said.

"You may need to go on the ground to stop Ta'ra opening the portal," Driar Yila said. "You see, the only way to enter the Faerie Realm is for a fairy or fae to open the portal themselves. They can open it in this dimension, or they can open it from the Second Dimension."

"And we suspect," Driar Brigel said, "that Astravar is using Ta'ra as a tool to enter the fairy realm."

"Which we cannot let happen," Driar Lonamm said.

I let out a long mewl to express my fear of this situation. Knowing that I might have to battle the demon chimera was bad enough. But now, it looked like I would also have to deal with over-sized wolves as well.

"Now," Driar Brigel said. "Does anyone have any idea how you're going to track the fairy?" He turned to Aleam with a smile. "Aleam, you're banned from answering this one."

Ange's hand immediately shot up. Driar Brigel glanced at her, but then turned his gaze towards her companion. "How about you, Rine?"

Rine shook his head. "Sorry, sir. I didn't have time to do any research." He gave Ange a nervous look.

"Very well. Seramina?"

She nodded. "I know, but you would rather the answer came from someone else."

"True, true," Driar Brigel said. "How about you, Ben?"

"Wait," I said. "I've seen this one on television. We listen out for tinkling bells, and then we walk anticlockwise around a ring of toad-stools and the little people appear."

Driar Brigel shook his head. "Not quite," he said. "Okay, Ange, what's the answer?"

Ange relaxed her arm, which had been stretched up towards the sky as if she'd been trying to reach a cloud. "Fairy dust... We look for signs of it glittering in the light."

Brigel nodded. "Always the diligent student, Initiate Ange. But that is the key, light. You look for golden glimmers in the sky when sunlight passes through it. You can't detect it when it's cloudy, and you can't detect it when it's dark."

"So what happens if it's cloudy then, sir?" I asked. "What do we do then?"

Driar Yila looked up at the sun and shielded her eyes. "It won't be, cat. We've had our snow, now the days ahead will be clear as spring approaches."

"But how can you be so sure, ma'am?"

"Because we have mages across the realm," Driar Yila said, "who can accurately predict the weather. You ask too many questions, Initiate Ben, when you should be taking action."

I growled, and I turned away slightly. "So, the plan is to fly out, find Ta'ra, bring her back again, and not get eaten by wargs. Have I got that right?"

"You're a fast learner. Now, get out there and find Ta'ra." Driar Lonamm said, with a slightly cheeky grin. Although Driar Yila was still her harsh self, I think the other two members of the Council were warming to me.

I didn't waste another minute. "Come on then," I said to the others, and I sprinted off towards Salanraja's tower. As I went, I screamed out in my mind at my dragon, "*Wake up!*"

She wouldn't be happy to be jerked awake like that, but clearly time was of the essence.

18

FLIGHT OUT

I sprinted across the bailey and up the stairs to the tower, faster than anyone could run in this academy. None of the humans had flexible spines like mine which allowed me to leap in long strides across the terrain, and none of the cats here were as spry as old Ben. I didn't look around to see if any of the cats on crow-catching duty took notice, but I'm sure they all stopped in their tracks in admiration at my work. Here, the Bengal from another world, descendant of the great Asian leopard cat, was showing his abilities in full stride. They all, I was sure, had a lot to learn.

Salanraja was already awake in her chamber, her tail lowered to the ground, her weight on her haunches, ready to run forward out into the open air. I scrambled up her tail and took my position on her back. She ran out of the opening of her chamber, dropped ever so slightly and then unfurled her wings. We were soon soaring over the fields outside Dragonsbond Academy.

Finally, I'd escaped the lockdown. But instead of flapping her wings to gain momentum, Salanraja continued in a glide, circling slightly.

"*Why are you flying so slowly?*" I asked in my mind.

"*Have you forgotten, Bengie?*" she replied. "*We're flying as part of a team.*"

"*But why? We're not even close to our destination yet. Isn't it better to get there as fast as we can? We need to beat Ta'ra to the Willowed Woods so we can stop her.*"

"*Which is why we need to fly in formation,*" Salanraja said. "*We'll be faster that way.*"

I didn't know what the whiskers she was talking about, and I assumed it to be some kind of magic or something. Still, I guess this way Salanraja wouldn't try to pull all kinds of stunts, sending me tumbling around in her 'ribcage' of spikes that jutted out of the top of her body. I hated that.

I looked behind me to see Seramina's charcoal dragon launch itself from the bottom of the tower that rose above the keep. Unlike other dragon riders, she seemed to prefer to carry her staff in one hand by her side, rather than on her back. She brought her dragon around in a circle and then had him fly back up until he was level with Salanraja.

She glared at me from the saddle, without expression on her face, but still the fire burning in her eyes seemed to display their own kind of anger.

"*Her dragon, Hallinar, wants to express Seramina's disappointment in you,*" Salanraja said.

"*What did I do?*"

"*Seramina thinks she needs to watch over you in case Astravar finds his way into your head. You shouldn't venture too far from her.*"

I growled from deep within my stomach. I tried to stare back at her, but that gaze was too intense, and even from here I could see how that fire danced within her eyes.

"*I don't like the way she stares at me. It freaks me out.*"

"*But she needs to do that. Seramina needs to know when Astravar*" *is trying to get into your mind. We can't risk losing you to him. Not after what the crystal foretold about Astravar's demise."*

"But why can't you protect me from Astravar anymore? Didn't you say that was your job?"

Salanraja lowered her head from in front of me. *"I don't know. My bond should be powerful enough. But there's something else about your connection with Astravar that none of us can quite work out."*

"And Seramina can see inside my mind and know when Astravar is in there."

"That's the gift the crystals gave her," Salanraja said. *"Some say that when she becomes a Driar, she'll be one of the most powerful dragon riders of us all."*

From behind, there came a sudden roar, and two dragons shot out of the tower above the dormitories. The first was Initiate Rine's emerald Ishtkar, the other Ange's sapphire dragon, Quarl.

The two dragons rose into the air, corkscrewing around each other playfully. They swooped and dived, creating a display even more impressive than I'd seen during air shows in South Wales. You probably know the ones I mean, when those fast flying machines shoot through the air, making lots of noise and then swooping around, before they disappear again.

The two dragons soon reached us and took their places on Seramina's and Hallinar's left. That put Ishtkar and Rine on the left wing of the formation, and Salanraja and I on the right.

"I thought we were meant to be the leaders," I said.

"Far from it," Salanraja said. *"The strongest flier takes the front, meaning it's less work for the weaker fliers to cut through the air stream to keep up."*

"So, who's the strongest flier?" I asked, trying to work out whether it was Hallinar or Quarl. But it was neither, because soon a magnificent beast rose out of the keep tower. The famous white dragon, the

only one of that colour in Dragonsbond Academy – Aleam's dragon, Olan.

She flew in a straight line without wavering one bit, as precise as a hawk towards her target. Her wings kept a fluent rhythm that kept her at a steady height, and she pushed her way between Seramina and Ange to lead the formation.

Aleam looked back from his saddle at each of us in turn. While he always hobbled on the ground, in flight he looked like a young man in posture. It was almost as if he'd been born for the saddle.

Olan let out a roar, and the other dragons replied with an equally noble cry. We then turned west towards the setting sun. I kept on looking out for glimmers of gold, but it was quite hard to see anything with the sunlight burning in my sensitive eyes. Still, although I admittedly had the sharpest eyes out of anyone here – and that included the dragons – everyone else also kept watch for Ta'ra. But no one reported any sign of any fairy dust, and it wasn't long until day fell into night.

By that point, we were approaching some woods. These weren't the Willowed Woods yet, but instead contained silver birch and beech trees. Olan led the formation down to the ground, and I bristled as I watched us descend. *"What are we doing?"* I asked Salanraja. *"We can't stop now. We've not found Ta'ra yet."*

"And we certainly won't find her under cover of darkness," Salanraja replied. *"Plus, I'm sure you don't want to be camping out in the Willowed Woods."*

I remembered what the Council of Three had said about those evil wargs, and I shuddered when I thought about the huge evil wolves that hunted through day and night and killed everything that crossed their path. With them and the chimera of this world, I'd learned of two scarier beasts than the hippopotamus of the Savannah. When I returned home, I'd have some grand stories to tell the Savannah Cats, I was sure.

"*Fine, we should land,*" I said.

"*That's what we are doing,*" Salanraja replied.

"*But aren't I meant to be the one in charge here?*"

"*No, the crystal told you to choose the team, not to lead us all into darkness and get us killed. Trust Driar Aleam and Olan, Bengie. They know what they're doing.*"

I said nothing more, as I watched the ground approach through the darkness. The sky was dark now, but I could still see the ground through superior vision. Salanraja thudded against it, jolting me against her corridor of spikes. We landed just on the edge of the tree-line, which gave us suitable cover from the wind coming from that direction.

"*Ow,*" I said. "*I thought you said you'd get easier on the landings.*"

She chuckled in my mind but said nothing else. So, I thought I'd leave that dragon to converse with her own kind. I scurried down her tail and onto the ground.

I decided to patrol the area and spray everywhere I could, just in case any cats in the area thought this territory was their own. Seramina continued to watch me as she climbed down the side of her dragon, who had flattened himself against the ground. With the way her fiery stare bored into me as she descended, I guessed it wouldn't be smart to go far.

LOVE LESSON

I t was winter and the night was cold. But this wasn't such a bad thing, because it meant it didn't take Rine and Ange long to set up the fire. They'd already brought firewood in the panniers on their dragons. The two older Initiates did all the work, while Seramina just stood as close to me as possible, with that same smell about her again of snowdrops and early spring. She continued to stare at me, but I tried not to let her weirdness get to me, and instead I curled up on the ground and tried to get some sleep.

But that was the thing – even in the land of dreams she was there, still staring at me with those fiery eyes. Except here she wore a white chiffon dress rather than her fur-collared coat. There was no escape. It was worse than having Astravar following me. At least the warlock gave me some moments of respite.

"Can't you just pretend not to be there?" I asked her. "You're going to turn me into a loony cat at this rate."

I'd seen a cat like that before – one of the strays in the neighbourhood who couldn't stand her loneliness. She would yowl into the night while she chased her tail around and around, and she would not stop yowling and chasing her tail until the day broke.

Humans would throw things out of the window at her, forcing her to scurry away to a different spot and yowl some more. But though humans couldn't hear her at her new location, I could from my sleeping spot in the utility.

On those rare nights when the master and the mistress let me roam outside – or should I say I failed to come in when called – I'd watch the mad cat dancing around beneath my perch on the garden fence, as if she had nothing better to do in the whole wide world.

In my dream, I realised I was chasing my tail, just like that loony cat. I stopped myself, slightly embarrassed. Then I wondered what I had to be embarrassed about. It was only me in the dream and this weird teenager who stood stonelike, not even blinking.

"You don't say much, do you?" I said, and I wondered for a moment if she was frozen in time. I couldn't smell her. Instead, I could smell raw lamb coming from somewhere.

"I know you don't like me," she replied, and only her lips and the muscles of her cheeks moved as she spoke. She had her hands folded below her waist, her chiffon dress blowing in the light breeze. "But this is what I have to do. To observe and protect you."

I growled, and then I realised I didn't even want to be in this dream. Besides, something was pulling me out of it, and I don't know if it was the roar of the campfire, the heat coming off it, or the rich scent of smoky lamb seeping into my nostrils.

I awoke to the brightness of the flames, and I turned to see Seramina looking down at me, standing in exactly the same posture as she had in her dream. I wasn't sure what I saw in her fiery eyes – was it the reflection of the fire, or were they just burning on their own accord?

A little away from the fire, the five dragons had all gathered in a circle and they were toasting massive lamb sausages on the ground using their flames. From behind us, the wind swished through the woods.

I turned around again to see Rine and Ange sitting next to each other, laughing as they held large sticks with their smaller sausages at the other end of them over the fire. They didn't have that awkward distance between them anymore, so at least something good was coming out of this trip. Aleam sat next to Ange, watching his sausage as it sizzled over the fire.

I stood up and shook myself off, and then I walked over to Aleam. I meowed at him, because that sausage just smelled so good. He laughed.

"Well, I thought you might want some as well, Ben," he said. He had one already prepared on the log just next to him, and he threw this down to me.

I mewled again in appreciation, and then I devoured the sausage. It must have gone down in five mouthfuls, before I was licking my lips and looking back up at Aleam.

"What? You're not telling me you want another?" he asked.

I gave Aleam the cute wide-eyes treatment and meowed again. Honestly, it was great to be able to speak the human language, but endearing gestures were often much better ways of getting what I wanted. Aleam laughed, and he took another sausage from a basket placed beside him and threw it to the ground.

Two grand lamb sausages were enough for a great mighty Bengal like me. I stepped away from the few morsels I'd left on the ground, richly satisfied. I turned back to Rine and Ange, purring. For a moment, I wanted to go over and sit on Ange's lap. But I could see they were getting on so well now I didn't want to ruin the moment for them.

Thing is, with Aleam sitting next to them, and Seramina not far away, they didn't really have enough privacy to get romantic. If only I could find a way to get Aleam and Seramina away. I could demand that I needed a toilet break perhaps. But that wouldn't get both of them away. Or perhaps I could think of another good reason as to why Aleam, Seramina I should go for a walk in the woods. Honestly, I was out of ideas.

Fortunately, though, this time Rine took the initiative and stood up, stretching his arms up to the sky. Firelight danced in his eyes, and I could see the joy in them. "I'm going to go for a walk," he said, and he picked up his staff from the floor. "Want to come, Ange?"

Ange looked around, and then her gaze fell on me. I made a motion with my head to tell her to follow him. Only good things could come from it. She looked a little sheepish and then turned back to Rine and shrugged. "I guess it's always good to walk off our meal before bedtime."

They didn't hold hands as they walked off into the darkness, but there was a certain skip in Rine's step, and I could hear in Ange's tone of voice how much she was enjoying herself. I moved over to the spot where Rine had sat – kept nice and warm for me, and I perked up my ears so I could listen to what they were talking about.

I could hear Rine's and Ange's footsteps rustling over the crunchy frozen leaves, as Ange chatted away. She was talking about Rine's and Ange's life back in Cimlean city. His mother had been the royal seamstress, apparently, and Ange's father was a baker in town. Rine and Ange had known each other for a long, long time, and they shared anecdotes from their childhood far too boring for me to recite.

Seramina glided over to stand next to me. "You shouldn't eavesdrop, you know."

"Shhh," I replied. "This conversation is very important. The fate of the world depends on it."

"No, it doesn't," Seramina said.

I glared at her. "You're only thirteen, I wouldn't expect you to understand."

"And how old are you? Five?"

Whiskers, how did she know? It didn't matter. "I said be quiet... Please."

Fortunately, Seramina's rude interruption didn't get in the way of the important part of their conversation.

"You know, Rine, it's been a while since we could talk like this," Ange said after a moment. "I forgot how fun it is, talking to you."

"You've been so wrapped up in your studies, Ange," Rine replied. "I think you've forgotten what it's like to have fun."

Although Rine's tone sounded jovial, it caused Ange to let out a sigh. "I guess you're right, in a way," she said, and she hesitated. "But if I don't get good grades, I won't be able to help my father pay off his debts to the moneylenders."

"I told you before," Rine said. "My parents can give him the money."

"No... We've talked about this. I wouldn't want that, and neither would my father."

"Fine," Rine said, and the conversation paused for a while.

"You know," Ange said after a moment. "I remember the days that you, me, and Bellari used to be good friends. I don't know what happened to them."

"It's not your fault," Rine said. "Bellari has just become a little insecure as of late. But she's a good person underneath it all."

"I know. I just wish she'd see I wasn't a threat to her."

Well, I knew exactly why Bellari saw her as a threat. They might have been old childhood friends, but they were both growing up and seeing each other in a new light. Unfortunately, neither of them seemed to realise this. I'd seen the way Rine looked at her, and I'd seen that demure expression on Ange's face when he did. But no matter how much I'd tried telling Rine that he actually liked Ange more than he liked his girlfriend, he never seemed to believe me. Perhaps, he thought me a little biased, which, in all honesty, I was.

"I'll talk to her," Rine said. "She'll come around, I'm sure she will."

The moon took the opportunity to peek out of the clouds just at that moment. It shone through the trees, framing the two in a silhouette as they stood facing each other. They were still standing too far apart. Things weren't working as they should.

"Why aren't they holding hands?" I asked Seramina. "They should be holding hands."

I saw her shake her head from the corner of my eye. "Maybe it's because they don't love each other."

"Of course they love each other. Why can't you see that?"

"You're a strange one," Seramina said.

"Shh. This is the moment. Ange is about to tell Rine what she feels about him."

She took a step towards him and put her hand on his arm. Rine didn't step away, which was a good thing. "Rine," she said. "There's something I wanted to ask you."

"What is it?"

"Are you happy? With Bellari, I mean..."

"Of course I am," he replied, and he didn't even take the time to think it through. "Bellari's so beautiful, and I'm the envy of all my friends. Plus, we get on well together, I think..."

My heart sank as I heard Rine say those things, and my dreams of living in a nice country cottage with Rine and Ange shattered into oblivion.

No! That wasn't how you did it, Rine. I'd seen the way these things work on those trashy soap operas that the mistress liked to watch back in South Wales. You spoke in soft voices. You complimented the lady. You smiled a lot. You moved closer and closer until it was time to secure your bond.

But you didn't, on all accounts, let her know there was another lady you were interested in. Otherwise, instead of kissing you, she'd end up screaming at you, and might even end up throwing something at you. And then there would be tears, and then the credits and the music would roll.

Human affairs were so complicated, which consequently made me happy to be a cat.

In the distance, Ange took a step back from Rine, and lowered her head. "I thought so," she said. "She is beautiful, I guess." She turned back towards us. "Come on, we should get some rest. We need to be sharp for the search tomorrow."

I'd seen enough of Rine messing things up completely. I took a mental note to have a word with him one day. Aleam was now sitting by the campfire, reading a book, clearly letting teenagers, cats, and dragons get on with their own affairs. I walked up to him and snuggled up beside him.

There was nothing else I could do for the humans this night and, more importantly, there was nothing else they could do for me.

20

THROUGH THE UNDERBRUSH

I didn't usually sleep so well through darkness. We cats are nocturnal after all, and our bodies have been designed for hunting at night. But that night, for some reason, I slept without waking. I don't think I even dreamed.

Dawn woke me as the sun came up bright and refreshing. It washed away the chill in the air. Though the snow had melted, frost limned the ground, evaporating under the spell of the sunlight. Aleam was the first to get up, and he handed out some breakfast of bread and sausages from the previous night. I didn't eat the bread, of course, but I wolfed down another sausage before we were on our dragons and flying out in formation again, Olan at the front, Ishtkar and Salanraja on both wings.

By this point, it had been around a day since Ta'ra had trans-formed into a fairy. Given her transformation only lasted a single day, she probably had reverted back to her normal form. Which meant that we also had to look out for a black cat. Saying that, though, she also might have used her final transformation. So, we had to look out for magical gold dust as well.

We weren't guaranteed to see either the traces of fairy dust or Ta'ra in her Cat Sidhe form en route. But Aleam knew the exact place Ta'ra had emerged from the portal. To return to the Second Dimension, she would need to either enter at the same spot, or have another fairy open the way on the other side for her. She would have no way of asking the fairies to open the portal on the other side, of course. So, we knew the only place she could possibly get in.

"*I saw you meddling in Rine's and Ange's affairs, last night,*" Salanraja said to me as we flew.

"*That's because they're going to be our master and mistress. The four of us will retire to a cottage, and we will have good lives without conflicts and warlocks.*"

A rumbling came from Salanraja's back beneath my feet. "*You do realise that they'd also need to keep their dragons outside that cottage.*"

"*So, we can all live there. In the countryside, with Ta'ra too once she becomes a cat, and lots of room to explore and hunt.*"

"*Really? And how will a small village in the countryside support three dragons?*"

I growled at her. Why did she have to be so practical all the time? "*I haven't any idea.*"

"*That's because your dream isn't particularly realistic, Bengie. Anyway, I thought you wanted to return home.*"

"*I do... If I can find anyone to open a portal, to my world. But I don't think that's going to happen.*"

"*It won't,*" Salanraja said. "*Meanwhile, you have a duty to Dragonsbond Academy, as do all the students here. By signing up, you pledged to serve them for a long time. Do you remember that?*"

I did, and I didn't particularly like it. Instead of answering Salanraja, I moved over to the gaps in between her spikes, and looked down from ahigh. Everything looked so insignificant from here – the sheep grazing in the fields, the scarecrows waving in the wind, the farmers cutting the grass with scythes, and that one black shape bounding through a yellow canola field, the crops rippling away from it as it ran.

"Wait... Salanraja, do you see that?"

"What?"

"There's something there, running through the field."

"You think it might be..."

"Let's go down for a closer look."

"I'll let the others know," Salanraja said, and then she swooped down away from the formation.

"Grasp her in your talons, Salanraja," I said.

"But it could be anything. Maybe just a goat skipping through the fields."

"No, that's a cat all right. Trust me, I know how cats move."

"I guess you would, being one."

"Exactly... You're so smart."

Salanraja soon caught up with the cat which had grown to be the size of a panther. It was Ta'ra all right. She was running so fast. But we'd both been so focused on the ground, that we hadn't noticed what she was running towards. A great forest of thorny, twisting plants loomed ahead of us.

"The Briared Woods," Salanraja said.

"Great... Another wonderfully original name."

Salanraja wasn't listening. *"Gracious demons, we have to act fast."*

"Then hurry."

"I'm doing so..." Suddenly her body lurched forward, throwing me against her back. I couldn't watch the ground coming so fast towards us, and so I held on with my claws for support. Salanraja never minded when I scratched anyway – her skin was so thick that I couldn't hurt her.

I peeked out from between the spikes, to see that the brambles were awfully close now. Salanraja suddenly jerked around, throwing me against the other side of her corridor of spikes.

Then she thudded against the ground, creating an awfully rough landing.

"*I thought we'd talked about the bad landings,*" I said to her.

"*Shut up, and go after her,*" Salanraja said. "*She's in the Briared Woods.*"

I didn't waste another moment. I scrambled down Salanraja's tail and ran across the field she'd landed on, into the underbrush. The thorns scratched, and they scraped, but I didn't have time to avoid them as I weaved my way through the thicket. I couldn't see Ta'ra, but I could smell her. The thick tangle of branches cut off the wind, meaning her scent hung in the air.

I took the straightest path I could, and I must have been running for about a minute, when I heard his voice in my head. Astravar was laughing like a maniac. Seramina had stopped him doing this in my dreams for quite a while. But I guessed she now didn't have a line of sight to me through the underbrush, so she couldn't protect me anymore.

"*Dragoncat,*" the warlock said in my head. "*You can't stop fate, you know. I will destroy this world, and the others, and you will be my aide.*"

"*Never!*" I replied to him. "*You can't take Ta'ra away from us.*"

"*Oh, but I already have. She will open the door to me to the Faerie Realm and through clever magic all the fairies shall become my pawns.*"

I really hadn't missed Astravar, and the last thing I wanted to listen to right now was his ugly voice. So, I blocked him out, trying to ignore him, to pretend he wasn't there. Those hideous cackles followed me everywhere though, and they made me want to halt in my tracks and give up the chase.

Still, I found my way through the brambles to the other side. Scratched and tender, I emerged into a clearing framed by willow trees. Ta'ra stood by a thick bole, a good minute's sprint away. Dark, sleepy shadows filled the gaps between the trees, twisting as if they had a life of their own. From the distance, in all directions, the icy wind carried a grating chorus of deep howls, barks, and growls. I shuddered, as the realisation came over me. I was surrounded by those hideous wargs. I could hear and smell that there were a lot of them, circling us from somewhere beyond the distant trees.

But I didn't have time to worry about them now. If I woke Ta'ra, she and I could fight them together. She could change her size and become a massive cat and toss them into the air. Thus, I summoned the energy I needed and dashed towards Ta'ra at full sprint.

"Ta'ra," I shouted. "Wake up, will you?"

As I got closer, she turned to me and looked at me with her eyes closed. She had shrunk to the size of a normal cat and I thought I might be able to swipe her out of her sleep with my paw. But I was sprinting so fast, and she just stepped away. I barrelled into the tree trunk and whined as I hit it head on.

I saw stars and my head thumped as I turned around. I tried to see behind the blotches of blue that marred my vision. They faded away after a moment, and then everything fell to silence. The absence of noise, the opening of a portal – I'd experienced it more than once. Static pulled on the hairs of my back, and the shimmering oval revealed a world as verdant as this one, except each tree, each strand of grass, the sky, and the clouds, were all painted in richer, much more vivid colours.

"Dragoncat, you seem great at survival," Ta'ra said, although she wasn't speaking her own words. "Let's see how well you do with my friends, the wargs."

"Ta'ra, no!" I screamed as she leaped into the portal, but it was too late to stop her. I summoned up my remaining energy and I bounded after her.

The portal closed before I could pass through it. The frozen willow leaves crunched underfoot, and then I heard the howls. I spun around, trying to identify the nearest threat, wondering where the wargs would emerge first. A purple mist enveloped the horizon behind the farthest trees. All around me, I could see shapes passing through this. They would flicker by like ghosts that only wanted to make their presence known for the briefest of moments.

But it wasn't long before I saw the first of the beasts, slaver dripping from its fangs. It approached me with a wicked grin, and the fury in its red eyes told me only one thing. It wanted to eat me whole.

21

WARGS AND WHIRLWINDS

My legs held me in place, not understanding what I wanted them to do. It was as if those red eyes of the massive beast had the power to paralyse. Yet it wasn't magic holding me in place, but my own fear.

A long crimson tongue lolled from the warg's mouth as it approached me. Its grin seemed frozen. It didn't charge yet, but rather sauntered up to me, its gaze affixed on mine. Then, as if to taunt me, it let out a loud bark, and snapped its jaws at me. That finally caused my legs to spring into action, and I scampered away.

I ran through the woods, Astravar's laughter echoing in my mind. *"Such a show, Dragoncat... Such a show..."* I sprinted faster than I'd ever known until my legs burned with acid, but I didn't let that stop me.

Another beast crashed through the woods ahead of me, blocking my path. I rolled to the side, tumbling over the crackling leaves. The purple mist creeped in ever faster, and I only just evaded the jaws of another warg that had emerged as if from nowhere.

How many of them were there? How would I stand a chance?

Then I remembered. I was a cat, and they were dogs. Which meant I had something they didn't have. I turned to see another warg charging at me. I ducked out of the way at the last minute, and then I made for the nearest tree. It didn't have low branches, but I didn't care at this point. I readied myself on my haunches, and I leaped up at the tree. I caught it with my claws, and I used all my strength to pull my lower legs away from a warg's gnashing teeth.

I scrambled away from the hideous growls, pulling myself up to the lowest branch. From there, I found a perch, as I looked down at what must have been a good two-dozen wargs, angrily circling the tree.

"*You'll never escape from me, Dragoncat,*" Astravar said in my mind. "*No matter where you are, I will always find you. I claimed you when I brought you into this world, and you'll end up serving me again with or without your own soul.*"

Beneath me, the purple mist seeped around the wargs. Wherever that mist went, dark magic also roamed. Which meant that Astravar or one of his more powerful minions was nearby.

Could the demon chimera climb this tree? I wondered. Had I just trapped myself with nowhere else to go?

I listened out for the dragons. They had to be nearby some-where. "*Salanraja,*" I called out in my mind. "*I need help!*"

It wasn't my dragon that replied, but Astravar.

"*Oh, did I fail to mention that little oversight? I've worked the magic inside you to create a little loophole. Now, whenever I'm in your mind, your dragon can't reach you. I'm afraid, right now, she has no way of knowing where you are.*"

Whiskers, I really was in a fix. Beneath me, on the ground, the wargs had stopped gnashing and trying to find their way up the trunk. Instead, they had arranged themselves in clusters of three forming a larger circle all around me.

One cluster had themselves crouched, as if ready to pounce.

They charged and rammed the trunk with their thick heads. Though the tree was sturdy, these beasts were also massive – even bigger than Great Danes – with an enormous bulk. Their combined weight rocked the tree like an earthquake, and I would have tumbled out if I hadn't had my claws fixed firmly into the wood. Still, the branches of the willow creaked, and they swayed slowly yet unnervingly.

Another cluster of wargs charged the tree, and the tree rocked again. I felt my branch begin to creak under my weight, and I scrambled further up the tree.

I looked back down at the wargs, feeling absolutely hopeless. Whiskers, this just wasn't fair. It was siege warfare, and I was the only creature remaining in the keep, absolutely defenceless.

Next, the wargs charged two clusters at a time. They hit the trunk from opposite directions, creating an impact that nearly jolted me off the tree. That was when I noticed something strange. Beneath the curtain of purple mist, I could faintly see the leaves moving. After a moment, they gathered momentum and seemed to rise as if whipped up by whirlwinds. More and more whirlwinds soon appeared, rising as great columns above the purple mist, which coalesced into the rough shape of a bulky humanoid. The mystical creature gathered even more power, snapping branches off the surrounding willows, gaining form as it spun towards me.

This must have been the anomaly which the Council of Three had sent Prefect Lars and Prefect Asinda out to investigate. Whatever it was, it seemed able to rip apart and gather substance from anything natural around it. It wouldn't be long, I realised, until it tore up my own tree, sending me tumbling to the ground.

The wargs crashed against the trunk again, and I groaned, not knowing whether I should scramble down and try to flee. Maybe, I could at least try to find the magical crystal that I guessed powered the magical creature behind those leaves. But I had no idea where to look for it, and if I returned to the ground, the wargs would tear me to pieces.

"*This is the power you are up against,*" Astravar chimed in my mind. "*And still, you have the arrogance to think you can beat me in mortal combat.*"

The stupidest thing right now would have been to let him taunt me. I needed to think of a way out of this. But Astravar was right, I didn't stand a chance. The branch beneath me creaked even more, and I knew it would be only minutes until it snapped.

If only I could fly like the dragons, then I could glide right over all of this. But then, this strange creature of leaves and wind could suck me into its centre where I would surely suffocate. It still was largely made up of whirling air, but it seemed to be gaining more and more mass sucked in from the forest. I would soon be part of that, compacted between a tangle of tree branches and leaves and soil.

I felt the branch snap, and then I felt it getting sucked in towards the golem. At the same time, I fell, and I caught myself with my claws as I dangled from the branch. As I struggled, the branch whirled towards the creature that had now become as big as one of the trees. I closed my eyes and prepared for the end.

"*Drop,*" Salanraja's voice came into my mind.

I didn't need to be told twice. I released my claws and fell, half expecting myself to tumble right into the merciless jaws of a warg. But at the very last moment, Salanraja swooped by underneath me. I landed right in her corridor of spikes and I grasped at her leathery hide with my claws.

I scrambled up to her neck to see that she was heading right into the centre of the forest golem. "*Salanraja, you'll kill us!*" I screamed out in her mind.

She ignored me and instead unleashed a torrent of flame. It lashed out all over the eddying tangle of leaves and branches and ignited the thing as a whole. Salanraja veered out of the way, and I clambered down a little so I could keep my balance. I turned to see the creature losing its power, as it raised up its arms into the sky and tossed back what I assumed to be its head and screeched like an angry dog on helium.

The whirlwind died to a tiny vortex, leaves fluttering out from it, and branches and twigs crashing down to ground, sending the wargs scattering. At the centre of the vortex, a small red crystal glinted in the firelight. This soon fell into the snapping jaws of a warg, who swallowed it, then whimpered and then scurried away. I took refuge in Salanraja's corridor of spikes, as she spiralled upwards. There, the dragons and the dragon riders were waiting for us, wheeling around the beautiful blue sky.

Olan looked down at Salanraja, and then let out a roar, as if to tell Astravar, wherever he was, that we would not be defeated. The rest of the dragons joined in the chorus.

Then, from a distant hill just at the edge of the Willowed Woods came another roar, ever so faint. Salanraja yanked her head in that direction, and I peered out from my roost at a jet of flame flaring out brightly against the dark rock.

"*Gracious demons,*" Salanraja said. "*Camillan and Shadorow are on that hill.*"

"*Who?*" I asked.

"*Lars' and Asinda's dragons. We're going there at once.*"

The dragons roared into the sky once again, and they quickly formed an arrowlike formation. Together, we shot off towards the signal.

22

PRISONERS

The signal had come from several miles away, and so it took us a while to reach the two prefects and their dragons. From far above the treeline, a bitter wind cut through my fur. I felt even colder when a grey and gravid cloud occluded the sun.

The pressure in the air pulled on my sinuses. If only I had made it through the portal after Ta'ra – the weather had looked pleasant in the Second Dimension, and I had seen no sign of wargs. I was also still worried about Ta'ra. What was Astravar planning for her, and when would she finally wake up?

The hill we approached was actually a small cliff made of sharp black rock that sprang out of the Willowed Woods. It wasn't particularly tall, but still the rock face was devoid of the trees, grass, or leaves that carpeted the land below. Well, I say devoid, but actually bits of branches and leaves and other stuff were strewn across the terrain, as if scattered by floodwater or a terrible storm.

We could see the two dragons on the hill. Asinda's dragon, Shadorow – a charcoal just like Seramina's dragon, Hallinar – was well camouflaged against the rock, but Lars' dragon, Camillan, stuck out like a lemon in a bowl of salmon. A little away from them, a primitive wooden cage structure, constructed of a mass of wiry branches, contained Prefect Lars and Asinda. We were too high up to see their faces, but I could tell they were sitting down and had little space to move.

"*What's wrong with the dragons?*" I asked Salanraja.

"*They were taken down by a forest golem. Those things, when they're massive enough, can throw tree trunks at dragons and knock them out of the sky.*"

"*So why did they need to signal us? I thought you dragons could communicate across great distances with your minds.*" Which consequently raised the question of why they didn't tell us where they were in the first place?

"*Astravar must have put some magic down to block that,*" Salanraja explained. "*There'll be a dark crystal down there somewhere. Their dragons told me that a crow visited for a moment, whom we suspect was Astravar.*"

"*What's a forest golem, anyway? And where is it now?*"

"*We just destroyed it. Can't you remember me burning it to a crisp?*"

"*That was a forest golem?*"

"*It was – one of the most dangerous golems in the realm.*"

"*But what you did was easy, and they had two dragons. How could that thing defeat them when all they need to do is flame it?*"

"*It wouldn't have been so easy if the golem had fully formed. Remember what you'd learned about golems in your Magical Creatures primers with Driar Lonamm.*"

Funnily enough, I'd been asleep through most of them. But interestingly, something came to mind. "*Golems gain strength as they gain more and more access to their source material.*"

"*Exactly. Golems at their very essence are just dark magical crystals with a spell cast on them to gather a certain natural resource in a specific way. They get stronger as they gain more of that element, but they also lose speed. Astravar must have ordered that forest golem to lose all its substance when you were stuck up in the tree because he wanted it to catch up to you fast. When it's just leaves and bits of loose wood, it's quite easy to set alight. But forest golems, when they become solid enough, are made of compacted wood and other forest material. They can destroy forests and grow so big they've been known to knock dragons out of the sky with their fists.*"

"*That doesn't explain why Lars' and Asinda's dragons couldn't set it alight.*"

"*Have you ever tried to set fire to a tree with a match?*" Salanraja asked.

"*I can't say I have,*" I replied. I'd never even tried to strike a match. It used to fascinate me when the master would rub one against the side of the matchbox to create a flame. But really, I'd never desired to light one myself. Who needs fire when you have humans to cook for you?

"*Well, just believe me when I tell you it's not easy. It takes a lot of concentrated fire to fell a fully formed forest golem. Usually, it's better just to fly by, or at least to send someone out to coat the thing in oil first.*"

"*I'm guessing then we brought lots of oil with us, given we knew we'd have to go up against golems?*"

"*Gracious demons, no. With the amount we'd need to bring, we'd never have made it here so fast.*"

I groaned, hating how confusing this world was. "*It still doesn't make sense. Those wargs would have beaten me out of the tree, eventually.*"

"*Or they would have just given up. Wargs are hardly the most patient of creatures.*"

My head was spinning by this point. There was a reason I always fell asleep in the Driars' lessons. All this stuff was so much to take in.

Us cats liked to learn useful things, like how to be stealthy as you padded the ground when hunting a mouse, as they could feel the vibrations beneath them. But when you were near a rabbit, you had to be quick, because they'd smell you before you even smelled them.

Never, though, would I have thought I'd need to contain knowledge about a creature that can suck huge tree parts and compact them into their body, then stomp you into the soil once they were done. Often, I still wondered if all this was just one big dream.

We'd pretty much reached the hill now, and the dragons descended. This time, Salanraja managed a gentle landing. Maybe she'd been listening to me after all.

The bare rock beneath her feet looked hoary, with patches of ice between the cracks. I didn't want to tread on that if I didn't have to. At least from up here, I had Salanraja's dragonfire warming my feet from deep inside her belly.

In fact, it was Ange who was the first to dismount her blue dragon, Quarl. The sapphire dragon first lay down on the ground, allowing Ange to clamber down out of the saddle. The Initiate took her staff off her back and she pointed it at the cage containing Prefect Lars and Prefect Asinda. A beam of green energy shot out of it and it hit the bars and spread out along them, giving the land beneath an eerie green glow. Presently, the bars curled away, leaving an opening at the top for Lars and Asinda to pull themselves out of.

"*I guess, when you're going up against a forest golem, it's best to take a leaf magic user with you,*" I said to Salanraja, proud that I'd finally learned something about this world.

"*Are you kidding? That's got to be the worst thing you can do?*"

"*What? Why?*"

"*Because leaf magic users are the first who a forest golem will target. It takes an awful lot of leaf magic to dismantle a forest golem, anyway. Only Driar Brigel is rumoured to have ever done so.*"

"*You mean I made a mistake asking Ange to come here?*"

"*No,*" Salanraja said. "*Because you at least didn't bring her here alone.*"

The two prefects stepped away from the cage, said thank you to Ange with a nod, and then walked over to Aleam and Rine, who were currently examining the fallen dragons. Ange followed them, whilst Seramina stayed in Hallinar's saddle, watching every move I made.

Though I didn't like the look of the sharp and icy ground, I was too curious about what was happening, so I scrambled down Salanraja's tail and went to join the other dragon riders. I looked back at Seramina when I did, wondering why she didn't dismount. But I couldn't stand her intense stare for long. It seemed to diminish the distance between the two of us and made me shudder within my skin.

Aleam was stooped over Camillan's wing, applying some white balm to a red gash that streaked through her thick yellow scales. The dragon groaned as Aleam massaged the wound, but she didn't scream out. "It will be a while until she can fly," Aleam said to Lars as he approached. "You're lucky to have survived this."

Lars bent down so that he could rub Camillan's forehead, causing the dragon to croon.

"How about Shadorow?" Asinda asked. She turned to Ange who was applying a similar balm to the charcoal dragon's wing.

"The wound didn't go as deep," Ange said. "But still, I think she needs to rest. Although Aleam hasn't had a chance to examine her yet."

Aleam shook his head. "You should have retreated, both of you. Two dragons and their riders are no match for a forest golem."

Lars shook his head. "There was nowhere to go. A line of bone dragons cut us off and pushed us right towards the golem. Astravar is in these woods, performing some kind of ceremony. We didn't know we'd be up against so much."

Rine lowered his head. "Astravar's here? But where?"

Prefect Lars pointed into the distance. "Just a few miles in that direction. There were bone dragons, a second forest golem, Manipulators, and a lot of activity until around an hour ago."

I didn't like the sound of that. "Why the whiskers would Astravar keep the bone dragons hidden from us?"

"Because he's planning an ambush," Aleam said, rubbing his chin. He turned to Rine. "There must be a dark magic crystal around here blocking any signals from the dragons. See if you can find it, Rine. Ben, help him out, will you?"

I mewled happily. Hunting things was my forte, although I wish Aleam had sent me chasing after a mouse or bird rather than a crystal. My whiskers detected some strange vibrations in the air, coming from a good hundred spine-spans away. I followed the resonating currents, tracing the crystal like one of those funny machines for finding metal that I'd seen the master and mistress' son using in the back garden of my South Wales home.

It didn't take me long to find it. When I got close enough, I also noticed it emanated a faint whiff of rotten vegetable juice. It stank so much that part of me didn't even want to go near it. But I braved the smell and lifted it up in my mouth, noting it didn't taste the same way it smelled. It didn't taste of anything, in fact, but it did warm my tongue though, as I took it over to Aleam and dropped it by his feet.

"Well, that was easy," Aleam said. He stepped back from it, took his staff off his back, pointed it at the crystal, and then he muttered something in a foreign language to me.

The ancient tongue of the crystals was about the only language I couldn't comprehend here. My crystal had gifted me with the ability to speak the language of all living creatures. But crystals weren't living and weren't creatures.

A single spark leaped out of his staff and hit the crystal, which shattered into what must have been a thousand sharp shards. A wisp of smoke rose from the remains of it, but the magic wasn't over yet. The smoke warped into the shape of Astravar's face, the noxious gas twisting his features and making him look even uglier than he was.

"Well, Aleam," the warlock said faintly. "I thought I'd at least be through the portal before I sent my ambush. But I guess I can't have everything perfect. Regardless, you are already too late." His annoying laughter followed his words, before the smoke dissipated.

In the distance, from the Willowed Woods, came a horrible high-pitched screeching noise that forced my ears down against my head to protect them.

Then, ten bone dragons shot up from the trees and into the sky.

23

SPELLS AND A PORTAL

Though Aleam was an old man, he was still incredibly fast to react to the first sign of danger. He stood up immediately and left the two dragons lying on the ground. "Lars, you jump on Olan with me. Asinda, get on Quarl with Ange."

Ange and Rine were already rushing towards their dragons. The two prefects didn't even hesitate to question Aleam's orders. They immediately took off, leaving their dragons behind, as they ran towards their assigned mounts.

Which, in all honesty, surprised me. *"Didn't you say it was worse than cheating for a rider to mount another dragon?"* I asked Salanraja.

"We don't have time to worry about ethics right now, Bengie. Get on my back." I stalked over to her, and I examined her tail swishing gently against the ground.

"Please tell me we're going to stay in the air," I said. *"I'd feel much safer up there."*

"No, you're all going to fight on the ground while all the dragons

battle the bone dragons from above. But we've got to get there first. Now stop wasting time and jump on."

"I don't want to."

"Would you rather I roasted you here and now?"

I growled, as smoke rose from Salanraja's nostrils. Olan had already taken off into the air, and the ground cracked as Ishtkar, Hallinar, and Quarl took off in sync behind her.

"Fine," I said. "But I'm not going to be the only one fighting the Manipulators this time, am I?"

"Of course not. Now, you have three seconds before I take off, leaving a smouldering cat on the ground."

I growled again, and then I ran up her tail. I secured myself in place in her corridor of spikes, digging the claws on all four of my feet into her leathery hide as she vaulted into the sky. She didn't seem to care about being gentle this time, but she had to catch up with the other riders after all. Olan led the way, with the other dragons flying right behind her. Salanraja soon caught up to them, and it was a matter of minutes before the bone dragons were upon us.

They came in from the flanks, to which Aleam raised his staff and he whirled it above his head. Sparks flew out in all directions, but they didn't hit us. Instead, they lashed out at the bone dragons, and froze them in place for a moment, leaving them soaring towards the ground, their spiny wings stretched out, with electricity pulsing at their wing tips.

Aleam's spell wouldn't last for long, but it was long enough for the dragons to lower themselves towards the woods.

We headed towards a grassy clearing cut into the trees, where Astravar stood surrounded by maybe twenty Manipulators, who fed the energy into their bone dragons using their ethereal staffs. These wispy creatures floated around Astravar, whilst a massive wooden giant with glowing green eyes and whirlwinds of fire dancing below its midriff, loomed even closer to the warlock. Salanraja had been right – its fists looked almost as large as a dragon, and it was tall enough to knock even Olan out of the sky.

A white glowing portal towered over Astravar, shimmering in the air but not yet open and displaying the world beyond. The warlock fed energy into this from his staff, and he didn't seem worried about any of us being there at all. Between him and the portal, a hollowed-out tree stump contained a purple crystal almost as large as my crystal. This glowed with a faint purple light, and as it made me feel terrible to look at it, as if it had the power to sap out my soul. The demon chimera was there too, walking widdershins around the tree stump and crystal, as if performing some kind of ritual.

I figured Ta'ra was standing on the other side of that portal, with the key to let Astravar in. If only she knew how much trouble she was going to cause. If only I was there with her, I'd find a way to stop her, I was sure.

Salanraja lurched forwards suddenly, and I used the strength in my legs to keep me on her back without flying off. Together the dragons veered towards the ground. All the dragons but Olan landed only briefly, and the Initiates and Prefects rolled off their dragons' saddles in a well-practiced motion. Salanraja landed next, and she lowered her tail, so I could rush down to the bottom.

The wind gusted against me as she lifted back into the sky. The leaves danced around me on the ground, and I peered through them to see Aleam clambering down from Olan's saddle. As soon as he was off of it, the great white dragon lifted into the air. Presently, an ear-piercing screeching came from above. The bone dragons had returned for another pass.

We were still in the woods, surrounded by willow trees with thick boles. The roaring of the magic feeding the bone dragons from the Manipulators and of a waterfall cascading in the distance, made the whole scene seem to brim with fury. Aleam summoned us together, and I didn't hesitate to join him. Everyone, except I, lifted their staffs off the ground, and each one glowed with the magic of their respective colours.

It wasn't fair, really. I was the only one unable to cast magic, and everyone seemed to still expect me to fight. I was half tempted to run away into the woods and never to return to these people. But running away had done me no good last time.

"Go for the Manipulators," Aleam said. "Once they and the bone dragons are down, then the dragons can work on the golem."

Well, that was reassuring. I guess there were now enough dragons here to ignite it with concentrated dragon flame, which meant forest golems weren't invulnerable. Yet still, it looked like we were vastly outnumbered.

"What about me?" I asked. "What should I do?"

No one answered, because Aleam was already screaming out and charging, all the students not far behind him. He sprayed out lightning magic from his staff, which danced across the landscape. One spark latched onto a Manipulator, freezing its action in time. The beam cut off from it, leaving the Manipulator's respective bone dragon open to attack by flame from Salanraja and Olan in tandem.

Meanwhile, Ange pointed her staff at a cluster of leaves and used it to cut off a stream of magic linking a nearby Manipulator with its bone dragon. Above it, Quarl doused the same bone dragon in fire, reducing the skeletal creature to ash.

Rine had ice magic, and he used this to create a massive frozen crystal that floated right in front of a Manipulator's beam. The white light used to feed the bone dragon shone through it and dispersed into a wide rainbow, making the beam useless. Ishtkar could then finish the bone dragon off in the sky.

Asinda was a fire mage, and so she sent out torrents of flame towards another Manipulator, in an attempt to set the ground around it on fire. It seemed to work quite well, and eventually the heat rising from the column of flame became too much for Asinda's ethereal target. The crystal at the centre of the Manipulator fell to the ground, lifeless, and Olan took down another bone dragon.

As for Seramina, I hadn't imagined that she'd be able to fight these things with her mind magic. But strangely, she used her staff to leach all the glowing light away from a Manipulator, sucking it into her staff. Then, she pointed this up into the air, targeting a bone dragon swooping down in pursuit of Hallinar. She let out all the energy that the crystal in her staff had contained, reducing the bone dragon to splinters that tumbled down from the sky.

I'd never actually considered what Prefect Lars' discipline was. He had a white crystal on his staff, which he spun around his body in a complex motion to create a magical shield dome. This surrounded Aleam, the students, and I. Some Manipulators now cast magic at us. They used their staffs to summon hideous Mandragora plants with jaws and thorny tendrils that snapped around us, sending up purple mist as they moved. But nothing could break the shield barrier that protected us.

Behind all this, the forest golem lumbered towards us. But by this time, the bone dragons and Manipulators had all been defeated, and our dragons attacked. The golem swung back at them with its mighty fists, but the dragons hovered around the lumbering beast, unleashing their flames upon it. Salanraja was right, it didn't burn immediately. But the golem's swings were slow, and the dragons were agile.

It was only a matter of time before the massive creation erupted into flames, sending up a roar like that sounded like a thousand scary fireworks – the kind that scream as they whirl into the night and then just explode.

"No!" Seramina screamed out. "He's getting away."

While the battle had raged, Astravar hadn't faltered from his work. Suddenly, the portal flared white, and soon after the light faded until it was only glowing around the rim. The portal now revealed the Second Dimension, that beautiful land where the plants carried a sheen containing every colour of the rainbow. Astravar whistled through two fingers, and his demon chimera Maine Coon bounded up to him. The warlock jumped on his mount's back and the chimera charged. It lowered its goat's head as if ramming something, and the snake tail lashed behind the demon chimera as it went.

Once they were a safe distance inside the other realm, Astravar turned around and pointed his staff at the massive purple crystal in the tree stump. His magic lifted it out of its perch.

The portal cackled with energy, and I knew it was only a matter of time before it would close. On the other side stood the demon chimera, my worst nemesis. But I couldn't let Astravar get away.

"Prefect Lars, lower the shield!" I shouted.

"What?"

"Just do it!"

He seemed to understand what I was getting at, and the shield flickered away.

I swallowed my fears, and I sprinted towards the portal. I dodged out of the way of the crashing, flaming foot of the forest golem as I went. Passing through the barrier between worlds felt like passing through the skin of a fiery bubble. It burned my eyes, and my hair was standing on end when I reached the other side. Then, my skin prickled even more as the portal closed behind me, trapping me in a foreign land.

The first thing I saw in the unknown world was Astravar on the demon chimera, bounding off into a forest of green spruce and fir with that purple crystal floating behind him that he'd carried into this world with his magic.

The second thing – or should I say creature – I saw was Ta'ra.

24

CATFIGHT

It wasn't just the sudden surprise of seeing Ta'ra there that disorientated me, but I'd also stepped from the winter into an intense and humid summer heat. The sun blazed down from an empty sky, and birds chittered all around us. I felt, in a way, I should be out hunting. Part of me wanted to just hide under the shade in this weather as well. But I knew I had to do something about Ta'ra. I couldn't let her get away again.

Ta'ra's eyes were still closed, and she faced me and hissed at me, displaying sharp fangs. I could smell raw meat on her breath, and I wondered if Astravar had hypnotised her into eating a rabbit just like he had with me many moons ago. Ta'ra was the same size as me still, and I worried she might become twice my size or even larger and devour me whole. She expressed anger, much of it, and it took me a moment to realise that this wasn't actually her anger but Astravar, who had taken control of her body.

"Dragoncat," he said through Ta'ra's mouth. "You weren't meant to come here. Everywhere I go, you seem to want to meddle with my plans."

"Just open up a portal back to my home, and you won't have to deal with me anymore."

Ta'ra opened her mouth and cackled in an unnervingly unfeline like way. "Do you really think I'm so stupid, Dragoncat? Our destinies are intertwined, and I need you somewhere I can keep an eye on you. If only you would see the advantages of the power I can give to you. You wouldn't have to go hungry again."

"Everything you want," I said, "is for your own selfish gain, Astravar."

"Coming from a naturally selfish creature himself. How would you behave, I wonder, if you had access to such power? You would never go hungry again."

"I never went hungry in my own world either. Until you yanked me across dimensions and forced me to fend for myself here."

"And I can make it worth your while, one day."

"No. I don't know what you're planning, Astravar. But I won't let you get Ta'ra involved in this."

"But why do you care about her so much?"

"Because she's of my own kin."

"Is she?"

I took a deep breath. "Whatever she was before, she's a cat now."

I was circling Ta'ra, growling at her, and I could feel the fury boiling within me. I was ready to fight for her freedom. It felt odd not to be able to look into her eyes as she bared her teeth at me, but I could imagine them green and glowing underneath her eyelids. Ta'ra was in there somewhere, and I needed to remind her of who she was.

"Very well," she – or rather Astravar – said in a deep growl. "I had hoped there would be a way of turning you over to my side with your soul intact. You'd be much more intelligent that way. Alas, it's not meant to be."

I readied myself to pounce, but Ta'ra beat me to it. As her body sailed towards me, I lifted myself up on my haunches and swiped back at her. I knocked her out of the way, and she whimpered and then turned back to me, a scratch visible on her cheek.

It was now my turn to pounce. I leapt at her, but she turned on her back and kicked me further along my path. When I turned back, growling and snarling, she was twice my size. She charged and knocked me to the ground. I tried to push her off of me, clawing and scrabbling, but she pinned me down by the shoulders.

"Wake up, Ta'ra!" I screamed. "Please, what do I have to do to snap you out of it?"

Still, it was no use. She couldn't hear me. She opened her mouth and leaned in to bite me. But as she did, her grip loosened, and I wriggled out of the way.

I didn't have any chance of waking her while fighting her, I realised. I'd tried it too many times now. So, instead of turning back to face her, I ran towards the spruce forest. I had a plan, and I hoped to cat heaven that it would work.

I had to slide to the side a few times, to stop Ta'ra catching up with me. She was bigger and hence faster than me. But this also made her a little clumsier to turn. I soon found a suitable target, a lonely fir tree, surrounded by a ring of spruces. Gold seemed to shimmer in its needles, and every inch of its bark seemed limned with the colours of the rainbow, like oil on water.

I leapt up the tree, sending Ta'ra crashing against the trunk. She must have hit her head so hard, because she took a while to collect herself. Maybe it had been enough to wake her. But, just in case, I clambered even further up the tree, its sticky sap clinging to my fur, and I leapt down at her from a branch. I used my momentum to swipe at her face with a soft paw.

I hit her, and she groaned in pain. She turned back to look at me with her bright, green, open eyes.

"Ben... What happened? Is this a dream?"

"You ran away and came here," I said. "You were sleepwalking. Or I guess sleep running..."

"I – Where am I?" She sounded a little confused as she turned her head to assess the surroundings. "This looks like home."

"We're in the Second Dimension. The Faerie Realm... Which yes, I guess it is your home."

She didn't quite look like she believed me. "Ben, this is a dream, isn't it?"

"No, Ta'ra. You were dreaming before, but you're not dreaming now. Did you see him in your dreams? Astravar..."

"That warlock? Yes, he was there, and now I'm just in another dream. I'll wake up soon."

She just wasn't getting it... I looked up at the glimmering specks of gold in the tree. The Council of Three had said that these were fairies. Were they up there, watching us from above? If so, why didn't they come down and say anything? Ta'ra surely was one of their own kind.

"Ta'ra... This is serious. It's not a dream, and I'm here in the Faerie Realm with you."

"But then, how did you get here?"

"Because you let me in, and not just me. You also opened the portal for Astravar, and he brought his demon chimera, and a massive purple crystal. I don't know what his plans are, but my crystal predicted the future, and it saw Astravar with an army of Cat Sidhe just like you, and he marched them towards Cimlean, and he turned some of you Cat Sidhe into fairies and made them explode, then he sent the rest of the Cat Sidhe in to destroy the city, and my crystal told me that this is how life, and all the food it brings us, could end."

While Ta'ra had looked incredulous before, she now looked absolutely dumbfounded. "Okay, hang on, hang on. Slow down, okay, Ben? I've just woken up from a terrible dream. I now have a pounding headache, and this is an awful lot to take in."

I mewled, and I rubbed against Ta'ra to comfort her, then I licked the side of her fur. "Okay," I said. "What do you want to know?"

She sat down, and I sat next to her. "Start from the beginning. Tell me exactly what you remember and take it slowly."

So, I did. I told her how she'd run away the first time, and I'd had to chase her until Seramina flew out on Hallinar and woke her up. That part, she said she remembered. She recalled how Captain Onus had locked her in the guard tower with no light in there, Ange cast some wards around the door, and then she went to sleep not knowing what would happen next. I then told her how she'd transformed into a fairy, and she'd said something to me when she was in her human form and then just vanished.

"Astravar made me use one of my lives?" she asked, with bitter undertones in her voice.

"He did..."

I next explained how she'd run away again, and no one knew where she'd gone until we found her bounding through a field of canola. I chased her into the woods, and I couldn't stop her passing through the portal. Then I fought the wargs, and I fought the golem, and I made sure that she understood how brave I was and what a hero I was. Salanraja then burnt the golem, I told her, and we found Asinda and Lars and their injured dragons. Then Astravar sprung an ambush, and we went to fight him too. I even took down a Manipulator of my own – I said – because she didn't need to know the truth of the story. Then, I saw Astravar was about to enter the portal, and I dashed through just before it closed. He ran away into the forest, and I fought Ta'ra, and I woke her up by jumping off this tree.

"Now," I said. "Here we are."

After I'd finished, Ta'ra rolled on the ground, and she started laughing. She tossed and turned as she did, clawing at the air like a maniac. I wondered if it was still Astravar inside her. Maybe he could also dominate her mind when she wasn't asleep.

"Ta'ra, please. Don't let him take control of you again."

She rolled back over and righted herself, her head high in the air. "This is such a wild dream. I must have eaten some funny mushrooms, really. Did you put something in my mackerel, Ben, without telling me about it?"

"I did nothing of the sort, Ta'ra. This is real, you have to believe me!"

"Okay, so let's pretend it is real. Then the next thing I should do is go to Faerini, my home city, and warn everyone. Because if it's all true, they're in a lot of danger."

"And if it's a dream?"

"I should probably do it anyway," she said, wistfully. "Then I'll wake up, of course, and I'll remember that I'll never see them again."

"So, let's go," I said. "And whatever you do, make sure you don't fall asleep again at all costs. Oh, but before we do, grooming time?"

"Sure."

I took some time to lick the pine sap off my fur in an attempt to get myself to smell less like a forest and more like a mighty Bengal again. Given how disgusting that stuff tasted, I knew I could never be dreaming. That's the law of dreams, nothing tastes so revolting in them you want to throw it up again.

We didn't groom ourselves for too long. Though hurrying goes against a cat's nature, we still had to do something about the whole saving the dimensions thing.

Thus, after we felt we'd struck a delicate balance between cleanliness and our mission to save the world, we sprang off into the distance towards Ta'ra's home.

25

REHYDRATION

I t was a long walk to the city, and though we tried to keep a good pace, part of me wanted to collapse against the ground and have a good sleep. I let out a few wide yawns on the way, and I must have almost dozed off while walking. Yet I realised that if I slept, Astravar could find his way inside my dreams again. He hadn't yet controlled me like he had controlled Ta'ra, but that didn't mean he couldn't.

The intense heat of the sun wasn't helping. Everywhere I went, I could hear water trickling, or cascading, or at least swishing. We passed some beautiful lakes, with reflections in which I could see my mighty face, clearer than in the mirror in the master and mistress' bedroom back home. Given the heat, part of me wanted to go for a long and refreshing swim. I don't think Ta'ra would have appreciated it, but like my ancestors, I didn't mind water just so long as it wasn't freezing cold. Some cats do, some cats don't; that's just the way it is.

Both Ta'ra and I were pretty thirsty though, so every now and again we stopped to have a drink of the freshest water I'd tasted in a long while. It tasted even better than the moat water in Dragonsbond Academy, in fact. Almost unnaturally so, as if the freshness had been magicked into it.

We talked about mine and Ta'ra's past, about our likes and dislikes, and about the future. I even asked a question I'd been wondering for an awful long time.

"Is it true, you really don't want to be a cat?"

Ta'ra stopped in her tracks then, and she studied me through the slits in her intense green eyes. "What does that actually mean?"

"Aleam tells me you'd rather return home, sometimes."

Ta'ra shook her head like a human would. Sometimes, her gestures seemed so strange that I wondered if I'd ever shake them out of her. "Of course I do. You don't lose your entire life, have it whisked away from you, and not want to return to it."

"Does that mean that if you were given the chance to change back, you would?" I thought about adding that Aleam thought he had found a cure. But I didn't feel ready to mention that yet.

"What's with the hundred questions, Ben?"

"I just want to know. Will you stay a cat or go back to being a fairy, Ta'ra?"

She turned up her nose and looked towards the lake. "I can't go back. Not for good."

"But if you could, would you?"

"Probably," she said. "So long as I had nothing to hold on to here."

I let out a long, sad mewl. I didn't want to hear that, although I also didn't quite understand why. Ta'ra turned to me, her eyes wide. "How about you, Ben... Would you return to your world, if someone gave you a chance?"

"Of course I would," I said. "I miss my salmon all too much."

"Is it just about the food?" she asked, brushing her nose against my chin.

"I also miss my master and my mistress, and the child too, I guess."

"Do you think they miss you?"

"They must do. I'm too cute not to be missed."

"I see..." Ta'ra lowered her head to the lake and took another lap of water. She turned back to me, the water dripping off her chin. "What if there was someone here who cared about you more than your master and mistress cared about you? Would you leave then?"

"Probably... I've sprayed my territory there."

"And what if there was someone in the First Dimension you cared about more than anyone else? Would you still leave?"

That caused me to pause. I thought about Salanraja, I thought about Ange and Rine, and about Aleam, and then about Ta'ra. How much did I care about them, really? I then thought about the delicious meal of smoked salmon and milk that Astravar had whisked me away from, and my mouth started watering.

"I still want to go home..."

Ta'ra turned away from me. "I see..." She stood up. "I guess we better be going then."

She strolled off around the lake, not looking back. It was almost as if I'd said something to offend her, but I couldn't think what. I let her go a little way, and then I rushed after her. "I thought you said it wasn't far."

"It's not," Ta'ra said, looking up at the sky where floating specks of gold shimmered. "In fact, we're already there."

"What the whiskers are you talking about, Ta'ra?"

She said something in her own language. Probably, if I wasn't able to understand her, I might have thought her language as beautiful. But instead, what she said translated to 'reveal big city before me'.

A glistening superstructure appeared out of nowhere. This wasn't just a city; it was one of the most beautiful things I'd ever seen. A mass of stone rising up out of the lake, with running water-falls which cascaded down from tall stone towers. The sun glinted off all the running and still water there, glistening as if off the facets of a crystal. Then, there was all the greenery – the wallflowers climbing up the stones, the huts set into trees and rock faces, the massive trees protecting the city underneath their wavering shadows.

Given how hot it was out here and how much shade would be in there, I knew where I wanted to be. But I was also absolutely shocked that a whole city had just appeared in front of my eyes. Was it really there? If I tried stepping onto the stones, would I fall to my death?

Ta'ra was studying me, and she'd clearly noticed my confusion.

"Has no one ever told you about glamour spells?" she asked. "Fairies like to hide things we don't want other people to find. Come on, this city doesn't bite." On that note, she skipped on ahead, and I cautiously followed her into the shaded streets of Faerini.

26

A PLACE OF GLAMOUR

P reviously, I'd lived in a village in the Brecon Beacons, in the Welsh wilderness where I could go out exploring whenever I pleased. I tried not to spend too long amidst the nettles and brambles – hating like any living creature to get stung and scratched.

Instead, I preferred using the time after the human tourists had left to explore the ruined castle on the hill. Tourists always left snacks behind, generous as they were. I appreciated the eggs and the bacon in the sandwiches, especially – even though our old neighbourhood Ragamuffin had warned us we shouldn't eat such fatty pork.

Hence, I'd never actually been in a city before. But then why would I want to? I'm a cat and I like my independence, thank you very much. I also don't see the point of trying to find my way through enormous crowds, risking my life every day near busy traffic junctions, and cockroaches and earwigs and the other nasty bugs which converge in such places.

I'd seen cities on television, of course – big ones where you couldn't see the walls, only vast glass and metallic towers stretching out as far as the screen could show. Who'd have thought that the first city I saw in my life wouldn't have been built by humans at all. And fairy cities were so different from human cities. Honestly, it wasn't clear in Faerini whether the forest was growing out of the city or the city was growing out of the forest. Probably, they were both growing out of each other.

Unlike Dragonsbond Academy, there were no gates into this place. But with the fairies' glamour magic, I guess they didn't need gates. They could just make their city disappear whenever they saw invaders on their doorsteps.

I had seen no sign of anything fierce, anyway. No dragons that could toast all the trees. No golems, or wargs, or evil warlocks who would surely love to claim such a magical place as their home. But now they had let one warlock into this realm, and I knew from experience how dangerous this warlock was.

We wandered through leafy streets. The houses were made of colourful planks of wood, sometimes built into the trees, or around the tree, or arranged across the branches in such a way that there was absolutely no way for it to fall. Really, this place made me wonder why I missed home so much. There was so much to explore here. So many trees from which to dash from limb to limb. So many places to hide.

We climbed up some stairs around one tree, ducked under tree roots, then passed over a cobbled passageway behind a rushing waterfall without even getting wet. The air tasted of pollen and good things, and with every step we passed bees carrying honey to and from their hives. A different bird song greeted us at every corner, but I couldn't see the birds and had to wonder if they actually had glamour spells on them too.

Though we passed many houses, nowhere did I see any sign of inhabitants. But I could make out traces of gold dust floating in the air everywhere I looked. It's weird – in a fairy city, I would have expected them to be darting around from tree dwelling to tree dwelling. Instead, I guess they had stopped to stare at a Bengal Cat that they'd never seen in this world.

"If these are little people," I said. "Why do they need such big houses?"

Ta'ra looked at me and laughed. "What would happen to a tiny collection of logs when you light a fire?"

"It would burn?"

"Exactly. Within seconds."

"That doesn't explain why you have such small creatures living in such big places."

"Because," Ta'ra said with a wink, "we can't have small fires when we want to cook. So, we need big cooking pots otherwise they'd get damaged by the fire. A big cooking pot, means we need a bigger fireplace to put it in. And can you imagine what would happen if you had a big fireplace in such a small house – it would burn down instantly."

"Can't you just use magic to cook stuff?"

"We don't have that kind of magic," Ta'ra explained. "Besides, we also like to have big places to have room to fly about. It also gives us plenty of places to hide."

"But you have glamour magic."

"Ah, but we need to be prepared for those times that glamour magic doesn't work."

"And so, everyone is hiding right now? Because I can't see anybody..."

"They're here," Ta'ra said. "But they're scared of us. We rarely see strangers here, and I was already cast out, if you remember my story?"

"But doesn't that mean they'll just cast you out again as soon as they notice you here?"

Ta'ra sniffed at the air and then took a deep breath. "Oh, I'm sure someone's sent an emissary to Prince Ta'lon to announce our arrival. We might see his soldiers at any time now. But until that point, I hope we have time..."

I didn't like the sound of having to deal with fairy soldiers. I know they were only tiny creatures anyway, and if they carried tiny swords, the worst they could do with them is fly up my nostrils and make me sneeze. But Ta'ra had said they could also cast magic, and if they could reveal an entire city out of nowhere, they might even be able to make an army of hippopotami appear in all these pretty ponds. Then we'd be in big trouble.

Ta'ra had now picked up the pace, and it was becoming a chore to keep up with her. I was already tired from almost being eaten by wargs. Meanwhile, Ta'ra had only just slept and she could at least have had some sympathy for my physical state.

"Where are we going?" I asked.

"To see someone." She seemed different all of a sudden. As if she no longer wanted to listen to me.

"Who?"

But Ta'ra didn't answer my question. She stopped outside a door of a hovel with a straw roof and rounded windows made of frosted glass. She lifted herself up on her hind paws, brushed away some dust from the door knocker which was shaped like a deer and made from wood, and she grabbed it in her mouth and released it, letting out a rap. "No metal here."

"Why not?"

She still wasn't listening. Instead, she purred and called out. "Grandfather? Are you in here?"

There was no answer.

"Grandfather?" Ta'ra said again.

Nothing.

Suddenly the door creaked open, and I jumped back, the hackles rising at the back of my neck. Out of the door came the whiff of rotten vegetable juice. Whiskers, Astravar. He must have been around here somewhere, or at least one of his minions.

"Ta'ra, be careful," I said.

But, still ignoring me, she was already pushing through the slight gap in the door. I groaned, and then followed her, expecting to be looking right at Astravar's cracked face. I only saw an empty home.

Everything was one room here, a bare fireplace with a pot over it for cooking, the smell of fruit rising from it. A cot wide enough for three small people to sleep on it – or for one cat to sprawl out across it. A kitchen area with garlic and dried herbs hanging over a window looking outside.

I wasn't looking at that. Rather, I was sniffing out, trying to identify where Astravar could be. It wasn't one of his minions here – it was the warlock himself, somewhere nearby. Yet there was no place in this room where he could hide, or at least he couldn't if he was in human form.

"I don't like this," I said. "We should leave, Ta'ra."

"Shush," Ta'ra said. She was scanning the room, looking for something. She peered under the bed, and then she jumped up on it, and patted down the mattress with her paws.

"Grandfather," she called. "If you're here, it's me, Ta'ra. I know I look different, but where are you hiding? I miss you."

My fur was standing on end at this point. There was something in the air here, and it wasn't just the smell. The crystal in my head was pulling at the bridge of my nose, throbbing there as if it wanted to return to its master. I turned in the direction it led me, looking at an empty doorway. There was nothing there.

"Ta'ra," I said. "Your grandfather's not here. But we need to get out of here, because Astravar is."

"Nonsense, if he was here, I'd smell him. All I can smell is the berry stew, and grandfather has only just cooked it."

I growled. "Ta'ra, how can you not smell him?"

She leaped off the bed and jumped up onto the wooden kitchen worktop. She pawed the garlic and dried herbs as if a fairy could hide there. "Grandfather... Where are you?"

I decided it better to leave, so at least I could keep watch outside. If Astravar wasn't here, he might be in the garden. I made towards the door, but a purple mist seeping out from behind it blocked me in my tracks.

Ta'ra laughed maniacally. I looked at her, thinking she'd gone mad. Next thing I knew, she'd be running around in circles on the floor. The laughter then came in my head and, as the mist gained density, I realised that Astravar's laugh also resounded from behind it.

"Oh, Grandfather, I'll find you eventually," she said. "And I'll find a way for you to lead the rest of the villagers to me willingly, I'm sure."

Whiskers, Astravar had gained control of her again. I backed away into the vacant fireplace and looked up the chimney, wondering if I'd be able to climb up it. Then, I realised the chimney probably wouldn't be the best place for a cat to be when facing off against a warlock, so I jumped up on the cot instead. Besides me, Ta'ra yawned and then started to groom herself on the countertop.

"Ta'ra," I said. "Snap out of it!"

She didn't even seem to hear me now. Astravar's cackling laugh got louder and louder, and he soon stepped in from behind the mist, his blue face seeming to glow slightly. "Ah, Dragoncat, I see you walked right into my trap."

I glanced back at Ta'ra. She had a glazed look in her eyes, and her pupils had become two black pools growing within ponds of green. I looked for a place to run. I could easily get past Astravar right now if he didn't send magic after me. I took a step forward before I heard a growling coming from the doorway.

The beast, my nemesis, stepped through the door. Its fiery tail hissed and lashed around at the air, spitting venom. The goat raised its head and let out a terrifying bleating sound, and then the Maine Coon part of the chimera opened its mouth and gave an incredibly loud and smelly roar. As the sound came out, the cracks in the demon chimera's body glowed, and I could feel the searing heat blazing out from beneath them. The eyes also took on a fire of their own, reminding me of Seramina.

Astravar moved over to the chimera and petted it on the head. "I can convert you to one of these as well, Dragoncat, if you like. All I need is a suitably venomous cobra, a goat, and you can take the part of the lion. Although, I believe you'll have the head of a Bengal, descendant of the great Asian leopard cat. Am I right?"

I didn't like being mocked. I turned around to Ta'ra again, who now had her eyelids shut. Whiskers, this had all been a ruse. She had just pretended to wake up, or Astravar had made her pretend to wake up. But she had always been in that dream.

I searched around the room, looking for a way out. The chimera was edging towards me, baring its teeth, while its snake tail bared even sharper teeth and hissed at me. I arched my back and hissed back. If I had to, I could take it down. I could clench my teeth around the snake and cut it in half. But then I'd surely die of its poison, and I didn't want that.

The demon Maine Coon chimera stalked up to me, and the fire raged in its eyes. "HELLCAT IS NOW EVEN GREATER HELLCAT!" it said, and this time I realised it was talking in the demon language – the same language that I'd used to command the demon dragon back into its portal. Maybe I had a chance.

Meanwhile, the crystal's lilting voice came back to my head. I remembered what it had told me, *"you must defeat the chimera."* This would be my moment of glory, and I knew exactly what to do.

"HELLCAT, I AM YOUR MASTER," I said. It had worked on the demon dragon, hopefully it would work on this too.

Nothing happened...

"HELLCAT NOT STUPID," the Maine Coon head said back to me. "MY MASTER FEED ME, AND YOU HAVE NO FOOD."

I growled. "What do you want of me, Astravar?"

Astravar let out a long sigh. "Just deal with him, Hellcat; we're wasting valuable time here."

"YES MASTER," the demon chimera replied, and it lowered its goat's head. Three scuffs with its hind hoof, and the thing was charging at me. It rammed the bedframe, which cracked in half, and sent me flying into the air. I landed just by Astravar's feet. He tried to stomp on me, but I rolled out of the way.

I heard the demon scuff its feet against the floor again, but I didn't want to hang around and let it kill me. Fortunately, the demon chimera had tossed me right by the door. I quickly scarpered out, back into the searing heat. As I went, something sharp lanced into my hind paw, and I felt a sudden pain searing through it. But it didn't stop me.

Astravar screamed out "Fool!" from behind me, but I wasn't sure if he was addressing me or his demon minion.

27

BLEARY

The snake head of the chimera had bitten me, and I knew it. I could feel the venom coursing through my muscles, and part of me wanted to just halt and give up. I didn't listen to that part of me.

Instead, I sprinted as fast as I could, maybe even faster than when I'd first left Astravar's tower. I didn't look back to see if the demon chimera was chasing after me. If it was, it would eat me. But if it wasn't, and I was lucky, maybe I'd find a suitable place to hide. I suspected Astravar wouldn't send it after me if he'd realised I'd been bitten. He probably thought I'd die anyway.

My muscles were cramping up from the venom that the snake head had injected me with, but still I ran. Water rushed by nearby, the sound of it hissing in my ears. My eyes had gone blurry, and my head was thumping, and I knew that if I didn't go somewhere soon, I would die here on this path for Astravar to find and do with me whatever he pleased.

Strangely though, Astravar wasn't inside my head. Even so, I felt a sinking feeling in my chest that told me I shouldn't have run. I was meant to be protecting Ta'ra. I'd come into the world to save her, and at the first sight of that demon chimera, I'd bolted. I was nothing more than a coward.

How I would become the hero who defeated Astravar and saved all the worlds from a fate worse than starvation, I had no idea.

It didn't matter, anyway, because I was going to die. The venom inside me was just too strong. But the last thing I wanted was for Astravar to find my body. He'd implied many times that he had a way of bringing me back from the dead. I imagined myself like one of those bone dragons, roaming the earth without a compartment for me to put my food in. Really, I couldn't think of anything worse.

Eventually, I couldn't run anymore, so my legs slowed. The world was spinning and whirling around me, and I found it hard to make out the shapes of anything. I didn't feel any pain anymore. I didn't feel any part of my body at all, in fact. It was as if I had disconnected from it completely. As if a part of me was rising to cat heaven, ready for those delicious meals of whatever they served you there.

But I couldn't let that happen. I was meant to be the hero. I wanted to reach out to Salanraja to ask for help. But she wasn't in this world. Here I would have to survive alone.

I looked around me for the sign of any shapes moving. There was nothing big enough to look like a demon chimera. Nothing had followed me. Yet I didn't really have control of my mind at the time to think that strange.

To my right, or at least I think it was my right, I thought I heard rushing water. It didn't give me a headache now. But it seemed to pull me towards it, and I passed through the cold cascade and found myself in a grotto.

The water sliced against the rock sending up a spray behind me. Seeking dryness and cover, I made my way to the darkest spot I could recognise, and I lay down. When I stopped, I could feel the venom raging through me once again, and I tried to keep my eyes open for as long as I could. Through the shapes, I thought I could see traces of something sparkling – glimmers of gold floating above my head.

Fairies...

"Are you there?" I said, and my words came out slurred. "Please, if you're there, I need your help. Your kin, Ta'ra, she's in trouble. Captured by an evil warlock. Please, if you can hear me, you must help."

I groaned as I mewled out the words. Then, the only bit of clarity in my mind made me realise I'd spoken in the human language. I needed to speak in the fairy tongue.

"Please, if you can hear me," I said in the right language, "you must help."

But no more words formed before my eyes became too heavy and I drifted off into oblivion.

28

BETWEEN TWO WORLDS

I f this was the end, I would no longer have a story to tell, and the future that the crystal had seen would not come to pass. But it wasn't quite the end, because I entered the dream world – that hideous place in the Wastelands where purple gas seeped out from the rents in the ground, and I could see Astravar's blue cracked head everywhere I turned. Purple fluffy clouds whirled around his head as he laughed, and he laughed, and he wouldn't stop.

"*It's not over yet, Dragoncat,*" he said repeatedly. "*Our destinies are intertwined.*"

But I was also somewhere else. I had a body in another world. There was a stinging pain in my back foot, and I groaned, and I tossed and turned. I probably had a fever, and I sweated through my paws.

Meanwhile, in the Wastelands, Manipulators rose out of the ground. Several golems also came out of the earth, formed out of hard rock. I coughed and sputtered at the gas that seeped into my lungs. It wanted to consume my life force. It wanted to dry me out to a desolate shell, an empty husk, a shell powered by nothing but dark magic.

Then Astravar, who knew where I was, could take my body and possess it. I'd come back to life without a soul, and I'd wreak carnage on this world together with his demon chimera and Cat Sidhe army.

This couldn't be how it ends. I had to fight it. I had to bring my body back to life. In the true world, I wriggled and squirmed and I did everything I could to wake myself up. My eyelids felt glued together. I tried to lift my head from the ground, pushed up against something solid, but it felt weighted down as if by lead. Alas, I was doomed to live forever in this hideous dream. I probably wouldn't even go to cat heaven. I didn't deserve it after all.

Astravar's magical creations had surrounded me now. There were too many of them to fight, and I had no choice but to back into a deep hollow in the ground. A golem made of the rock of the earth – even bigger than the forest golem that I'd battled with the wargs – now loomed over me. It had a massive fist of rock poised right above my body. It brought it down, ready to crush my bones into the earth as if the hollow was a mortar and its fist a pestle.

But I still had a little strength within me, and I used it to lift my head off the ground and open my impossibly heavy eyelids. My vision flooded with bright light.

29

FAERIE FOLK

I awoke, back in the real world, or at least the fairy world. Given all the glamour spells around here, I didn't actually know whether I was looking at reality or an illusion. An old wrinkly and slight man with a bandana around his head and a scraggly red beard was looking down at me. Something about him didn't look human. It was in his posture, I think – much as a wildcat doesn't behave the same way as a cat.

I backed away from him against the cold and slimy stone wall. It was covered in moss, and so I didn't stay long against it. I arched my back and watched this man or fairy or whatever he was, wide-eyed.

"Don't be scared," he said. "This is a safe place. We've hidden this grotto through glamour magic. Whatever hurt you won't find its way in."

I wanted to tell him that his magic was probably no match for a warlock like Astravar. But I realised if Astravar wanted to find me, he probably would have done so by now.

My back paw still stung a little, but there was also a slight tickle there, as if water was washing over it and soothing the pain. I looked back to see it glowing with a faint yellow light. In fact, my whole fur seemed to be glowing from the skin beneath.

"What did you do to me?" I asked.

"Some of us fairies also know the art of healing," the man said. "At least if we have the fairy dust donated to us from the right crystal. But alas, it's a dying art."

I took a step towards the man and sniffed his foot. He smelled of the berry soup in Ta'ra's home. "You're Ta'ra's grandfather..."

The fairy man waved his hand in front of him a few times and then gave a ridiculously drawn-out bow. "Be'las, at your service. And your name is Ben."

"How do you know?"

"Because I heard my granddaughter call you that when you were walking around outside."

"Then you'll know I'm a descendant of the great Asian wildcat."

"I didn't, but that's all well and good. I'm a fairy of Faerini, weaver of invisible silk and other kinds of magical thread."

Now I was getting the feeling he was pulling my leg. "I didn't see a spinning wheel in your house," I pointed out.

"That's because it's an invisible spinning wheel," Be'las said with a smirk. "How else do you think I weave invisible thread?"

"And who would need invisible thread?"

"Why, anyone who doesn't want to have their clothes noticed. This is fashionable in some parts."

I stalked around the grotto, sniffing out whoever else might have been here. There were certainly others – I could see bits of gold dust floating around in the air. "Why don't your friends show themselves?"

"They're rather shy. I'm the only one bold enough to represent them."

"Then why do you trust me?"

"Because you brought my granddaughter back, despite her hideous form and smell..."

"She looks a lot better than you do, old man!" In fact, I was grateful he wasn't wearing clothes made of his invisible thread.

"Now, now." Be'las stretched his arms out in front of him. "There's no need for that kind of behaviour. Us fairy folk are pleasant people, and we don't like insults."

I groaned. I thought humans were weird. "I thought Ta'ra was banished?"

The fairy man lowered his head. "Doesn't mean some of us didn't want her to stay. Ta'lon threw her out of the kingdom. But I've felt guilty every day since he did. I watched her go, and I did nothing. But now she's back, but she's not in a way, because when I saw you and her, I could tell she was under the warlock's control. That's why I didn't follow her, and we decided instead to hide here. What does Astravar want with us? We've always been a peaceful kingdom."

I rubbed myself against the man's leg, and he flinched and backed away from me. He seemed to think that I might want to do him harm. But then he was bigger than me, or was he? I didn't actually know. Eventually, though, he relaxed. There was a ledge of rock in the grotto, and so I leaped on to it and lay down on it. Then, I told him about my crystal and what it had forecast.

As I narrated, one by one, fairy folk appeared all around me. This should have startled me, but instead, it seemed perfectly natural. Whenever a fairy wanted to appear, the air shimmered around it, and there stood a man or woman – looking human except with funny postures and skin that glittered with specks of gold. They sat down on rocks and tree stumps and ledges scattered around the grotto.

There must have been a good fifty of them by the time I finished my story.

"He wants to turn everyone here into a Cat Sidhe just like Ta'ra," I said. "I ran after her, and everyone at Dragonsbond Academy tried to stop her from opening the portal. But now Astravar is in this world, and he wants to create an army to destroy every dimension. There would be no cats, no butterflies to chase, no salmon to eat from the bowl every morning. Our lives will be ruined."

A woman stepped forward. She wore a colourful dress, striped like the rainbow and flared at the bottom so that it showed her tall legs. Her golden hair spilled over her shoulders where it seemed to froth like waves.

That's when I noticed what was funny about them. These fairies didn't walk like a human or any creature that obeyed gravity should. Normal creatures lifted one foot, then fell on top of another foot, then pushed back against the fall to create continuous motion. But this fairy, and all the fairies as they moved, seemed to glide as if over ice. There seemed no friction between their feet and the ground at all.

"I am Go'na, Prince Ta'lon's sister," she said in an incredibly high-pitched voice that sounded like a cartoon mouse.

I'd already told them my name and ancestry, and so I didn't need to repeat it. "Why do you fairies have such strange names all the time?" I asked instead.

"I'm sorry," Go'na replied. "But I'd rather focus on the task at hand. If what you say is true, then I think Astravar must be heading to the palace now. He wants to use Ta'ra's love for Prince Ta'lon to cast a magic more powerful than anything we've ever imagined before." A tear came down the fairy's porcelain cheek, and she wiped it away.

I wasn't going to let fairy emotions impede the matter at hand – we had seven dimensions to protect. "Just lead me to the palace. Because we need to stop Astravar before it's too late."

Go'na sniffled and turned away. Be'las stepped forward. "Just follow us."

Before I could object, the air shimmered everywhere in the grotto and all I could see were those glistening specks of gold. But now I knew what to look for, I could track them as they floated through the waterfall.

I rushed through the water, and then I followed the fairies towards a massive tree in the centre of Faerini city that towered above everything else. Strangely, I could swear it hadn't been there before.

30

AN OAKEN PALACE

From a distance, the palace looked like a massive oak tree – kind of odd-looking, offset against all the pines and firs and spruces out here. As we got closer, it took on more of an ornate look. As Ta'ra had said, there was no metal in this world. Instead, it had these intricate woodcarvings etched into the tree bark, the wood of the doors, and decks leading out from the palace. They displayed winged humans in flight, carrying fruit and water, weaving clothes, and planting saplings in the forest. There was no one in battle, as I'd seen in some paintings around Dragonsbond Academy. Rather, the pictures showed the fairies going about their everyday lives.

The fairies – or at least the gold specks in the air representing them – had gathered around the large yellow door, which opened to display a spacious interior. The tree roots lunged out of the ground as if disturbed by massive waves. Once the door had opened, I saw these to be the wings of the palace, the corridors twisting around and up and down unlike any human construction. There was no plaster on the walls, or anything like that. Instead, the walls had a smooth yet unvarnished wooden texture, as if they had been thoroughly sanded down.

A cool breeze circled the interior of the tree, and it smelt glorious to be in here – with a rich natural aroma just like the garden I knew so well in South Wales. I thought it might be great fun to explore, but I knew we didn't have time.

Once we were inside the main atrium – a spacious room with a spiral staircase leading up the trunk, Be'las appeared to me in his human form. "The throne room is at the top," he said.

"All the way up there?" I asked. It led so far up I couldn't see where the staircase ended.

"We tend to fly up..."

"Well, that's all well and good if you can fly."

"Maybe you'll learn one day."

"I don't want to," I growled back. "I'm quite happy being a cat, thank you."

"Suit yourself," Be'las said. "I'll meet you at the top." The air around him shimmered.

"Wait!"

"What?" Be'las said, but he'd already vanished, and I couldn't quite make out which speck of floating gold he was.

"We should all go up the staircase together. What if there are guards?"

"Guards? We don't employ guards."

"What do you mean you don't have guards?"

"Haven't you worked it out yet? Why would we need guards when we have glamour magic? Besides, there's little in this world that's a threat to us, as the only way to enter the Faerie Realm from another dimension is for another fairy to open a portal."

"Or a fae..." I said, remembering how Aleam had told me once that faes were dark fairies.

"Faes don't come home very often. They're manipulated by

warlocks to attack the humans who oppose them in the First Dimension. The warlocks have always taken little interest in the Faerie Realm."

"Until now."

"Yes, until now."

"Then let's just go up..." I leaped up the stairs, trying to take them in as large strides as I could. Because I'm an energetic Bengal, I rarely run out of breath, so I thought this would be easy. As I went, the fairies flew around me in circles, as if they wanted to show off that they could fly so much faster than me.

Instinctively, I wanted to reach up and try to bat them out of the way. I found it disturbing with them continuously flitting past my vision when I was trying to get to the top as fast as possible. I resisted though, as I still suspected they could do even worse things with their magic, like turning me into a snail and making the climb even more difficult.

The staircase eventually curled into itself towards the centre of the oak trunk. It led to a large outcropping from the trunk and had a ceiling at the top. Another yellow, closed door stood at the top of the staircase, decorated with wood carvings of fairies flying around various flowers. Whoever was inside had sealed it shut, and it didn't seem to have any door handle to open it with. I tried pushing it, but even with my mighty Bengal strength I couldn't budge it.

I felt the air shift from behind me and then came the smell of ozone. Be'las stood there looking at the door as he shook his head. "It's usually open," he said. "Visitors are meant to be welcome at all times."

"Well, we might not be now," I said. "How do we open it?"

"We can't from here."

"What do you mean, can't?"

"The door can only be opened from the other side."

"Then we're going to have to break it down."

"You can't. It's sealed by protective magic."

Whiskers, I couldn't believe I was hearing this. I moved up to the door and took a deep breath so I could bellow out at the top of my lungs. "Ta'ra," I shouted. "Ta'ra, are you in there?"

No response.

"Prince Ta'lon," I tried. "Prince Ta'lon, I am Ben, a Bengal and descendant of the mighty Asian leopard cat. I also work for Dragonsbond Academy and I'm here to save the Faerie Realm. If you value your kingdom, it's essential you open this door at once."

Still nothing.

I turned back to Be'las, who had a confused frown on his face. "It isn't working," I said. "Maybe we need to say a magic word."

"Magic word?"

"I don't know, like 'open sesame'?" I checked to see if the word had had any effect. It hadn't.

"Why would I want to open a seed?" Be'las asked.

"You don't. You use the phrase to open mystical doors to places." That was one advantage of being taught the language of all creatures, the crystal had given me a whole host of magical words to try in multiple languages.

"Alacazam!" I tried.

Nothing happened.

"Abracadabra!"

Nothing.

"Sim-sala-bim!"

Still nothing.

"Whiskers, Astravar, open this bleeding door!"

Silence ensued. I turned, ready to leave, ready to give up. I had no choice; I'd be stuck in this world forever. But I didn't take a single step before the door creaked from behind me. I spun around to see the door rattle against its hinges a few times.

Then, it swung open, letting out an incredibly warm and putrid draft of air that smelled of – you guessed it – rotten vegetable juice.

Inside, Astravar sat on a throne wrapped in living flowers of all kinds of different colours. The demon chimera sat at the warlock's foot, panting heavily. The purple crystal that Astravar had brought into this world hovered just below the ceiling, infusing its surroundings with a faint purple light. Wooden columns propped up the throne room, each intricately decorated with images that didn't seem to belong here – images of massive cats tearing tiny cities to shreds, throwing towers into the air, and trampling houses and city walls. A purple mist seeped around these columns, and above this stood exactly what had I feared all this time...

An army of Cat Sidhe sat there, hypnotised with their eyelids sealed shut, arranged in neat columns as if ready to march into battle.

Whiskers! We'd arrived too late.

31

SPRUNG

A shiver ran down my spine and time seemed to stop for a moment, as I took in the contents of the room. Then, slowly, things happened.

The fairies, still golden glitters in the air, had already started floating into the room. They didn't seem to move with a will of their own anymore. Rather, they gravitated towards the crystal, which grew in luminosity as the fairies drew closer.

"Stop!" I shouted. "It's a trap!"

My words did nothing to stop the fairies, as they drifted closer and closer. They didn't even seem to have any fight in them – any will to draw themselves away from the hypnotic spell the crystal was casting on them. Astravar looked across the room with that horrible grin on his face. The demon chimera also lifted its head, and it blinked at me and yawned.

Still, Be'las stood behind me in his human form, his gaze transfixed on the crystal and his eyes wide. His expression reminded me of a kitten who'd just seen milk for the first time. Soon enough, the air shimmered around him, and he became a golden speck of dust, floating towards the crystal with his friends.

I glanced from the staircase to Astravar sitting there on the throne, one leg crossed over the other as he leant forward on his staff. My gut told me once again to flee. But last time I did that, the snake tail of the chimera had bitten me, and I'd almost died.

"Oh, come in Dragoncat," Astravar said. "Come on in."

Now he'd mentioned it, I didn't want to obey him either. So, I put my rear down on the ground and groomed myself.

"I said, come in, you impudent cat!"

Suddenly, I felt something grasp hold of my side. Astravar had shot a purple beam right towards me, and he used it to pull me into the room. I screeched, trying to use my front claws to keep purchase on the wooden bark beneath my feet. I held myself there for a while, Astravar's magic trying to tug me into the room. But force was too strong and the pain in my claws became too great. If I didn't let go, they would get torn out of their sockets.

I released my grip and screeched as Astravar magically dragged me across the floor. I skidded to a stop just underneath the crystal. A magical energy ball full of violet light pulsated around me. The only muscles I could move were those in my spine and neck, and so I looked up to see the fairies had now reached the crystal. One by one, each fairy got sucked in towards the surface of it, and then let off a bright spark of light.

They floated like dander to the floor, now bereft of that golden glimmer. As they landed, the mist creeped up to accept them. The purple gas shrouded them in a roughly humanoid shape. Beneath the mist, it looked like the air shimmered a little, and the fairies very faintly took their human glamour forms. Astravar waited until all the specks had fallen and no traces of gold remained in the air.

Then, he lifted himself off the throne, and he cackled loudly as he reached into the pouch on his hip to produce a handful of small glistening crystals. He threw these up at the large purple crystal, and he swung his staff around in one deft motion and shot out a purple beam. The smaller crystals leapt towards the beam like metal to a magnet, and a ball of light formed at the front of the beam, suspended just in front of the crystal.

Soon, Astravar cut off the beam, leaving the glowing ball remaining. The magical ball followed the slow and steady motion of his staff – the smaller crystals circling around it. The features on Astravar's face tightened into a mask of concentration. He opened his mouth and let out a tremendous yell. The ball shattered, sending the crystals out in many directions at once. Some spun across the floor and came to rest, but there were still enough remaining to shoot right into the foreheads of the fairies, each one creating a blue glowing spot.

I saw Go'na amongst them then, with her pretty wavy hair. Her eyes went from vibrant to white as the glow intensified on her forehead. The mist continued to rise around her, and then it changed shape, and Go'na transformed from human to feline. Her features warped and her clothes melted into her skin, which soon sprouted black fur.

When the transformation had ended, she had become a black cat with a white diamond crest on her chest, much like all the other fairies around her. Astravar lowered his staff.

"Excellent," he said, looking down at me, and he released the magical spell that had had me imprisoned. The violet ball surrounding me dimmed, and I could see clearly once more. I could also now speak.

"Astravar... What have you done?"

"What have I done?" Astravar said. "Oh, my dear servant, you have done this yourself. I only needed to set up the spell. Here, I used your friend Ta'ra to round up half the village. But you endeared the resistance to your cause and brought them to me. You only needed to present yourself to the rest of the villagers as an ally. What a wonderful gift this is, Dragoncat. And my demon chimera here didn't quite inject enough venom into you to kill you, clever minion that he is." He tickled the chimera under its Maine Coon head's chin.

I realised then that when Astravar had called out, "Fool!" before, it had been in fact intended for me. But it wasn't a call of anger. It had been a mocking remark – all a part of his little game.

The Cat Sidhes had now fully taken shape, and they moved into neat columns next to the others. They all had their eyes closed, but every one of them had their heads turned towards me. Remarkably, Astravar could control them all like this, and still function normally.

"You'll never get away with this, Astravar," I said. "Dragons-bond Academy will find a way to stop your schemes."

"Will it now?" Astravar said, his lips stretched into a grin so wide I wondered how his brittle-looking skin didn't crack. "You don't realise what I've just done, do you? I haven't just created an army from fairies, but extracted their magic from them, so I can use it as a reserve. With this," – he pointed up at the massive purple crystal suspended above my head – "I am now powerful enough to tear apart cities with magic alone. They can use my most powerful magic when they use a transformation. I've never realised until now how potent this fairy alteration magic is."

That explained, come to think of it, why in my crystal's vision Astravar had converted them into fairies to attack the dragons. The prediction must have seen them using so much magical power that they couldn't handle it, and so they then fell lifelessly to the floor.

"I shall stop you," I said. I also opened my mouth to tell him all that I'd seen in the crystal. But I thought better of it. Why give him information that he didn't have?

"Yes," Astravar said, his chin resting on steepled hands. "There is that issue of our destinies being intertwined. I can always kill you right now. That might solve my problem."

"Then what are you waiting for?" I asked, with a growl.

"Well," Astravar said, and he pointed his staff at the massive hovering crystal. "You see, I've had a bit of a problem since I brought my Hellcat into this world. When I took my little pet from the Seventh Dimension, I also took on a little debt with Ammit, the crocodile-hippo-lion demon goddess of the Seventh Dimension. And trust me, I don't want to leave a debt of such significance unpaid."

He put his hand underneath the demon chimera's chin and ruffled its mane. The chimera made a purring sound that sounded like rocks grating against each other. As Astravar stroked his pet, a purple beam came out of his staff towards the crystal. It entered it through one face, then emerged refracted on the other side, this time red.

Suddenly, it was as if time stopped. The world fell silent, if just for a moment. Then, a blast of heat came out from behind me, followed by an infernal roar. I looked over my shoulder at the portal that Astravar had summoned there. It led, I could see, into the fiery landscape of the Seventh Dimension.

"You plan to send me there?" I asked, and I mewled softly as I did so, because I really didn't want to go.

"Oh, no," Astravar said. "You're going to go willingly."

"Why the whiskers would I go there?"

"Because if you don't, then my demon chimera will rip you apart." He released his hand from the chimera's mane. "Devour him, Hellcat!"

The demon chimera let out a happy roar. It came out so loud that it shook the room, I swear. I tried to look around behind the portal, see if there was a way out from the other side of the room. But the Cat Sidhe army had each become the size of a panther, and they blocked the way out. In front of me, the Cat Sidhes also closed in, creating a corridor for the demon chimera to stalk down. Its snake tail whipped out at the air, its goat's head bleated at an ear-piercing pitch, and the Maine Coon's head licked its lips as I moved forward.

Maybe I could fight it. I'd need to attack the snake first. But my legs trembled as I tried to stay put and muster up the courage to battle the thing. The crystal can't have been serious, could it? How was I meant to beat something that was so much bigger than me and had three heads?

The chimera was now so close to me I could smell its rancid breath. It readied itself to pounce, and I could see in its eyes that it intended to eat me very soon. I knew I didn't have a chance against the demon chimera, and I hoped that in the Seventh Dimension I might at least live another hour.

Hence, I fled through the raging portal into the searing heat.

32

THE SEVENTH DIMENSION

I skidded to a stop right at the edge of a rock ledge. The ground was so rough, it seemed to tear my skin. I dug in my claws to the ground to stop myself from going over the edge, and then I groaned as I looked at the sea of boiling lava stretching out right to the horizon. It wasn't far beneath me, and bubbles rose from the molten sea, which I was sure would melt me alive.

I spun around, wanting to jump back into the Faerie Realm. Being eaten alive by a chimera might actually have been a better option than boiling to death here. But the portal had already vanished. Astravar had banished me to the Seventh Dimension, and it soon dawned on me that there was no turning back. A nauseous smell of rotten eggs followed me wherever I turned, and I found it hard not to vomit.

Fortunately, I wasn't stuck on an island surrounded by lava. I had just entered the land at what looked like the lowest point. As close as physically possible, in other words, to that bubbling sea.

Most of us cats were made to live in hot places, so in many ways

I might have done better in this place than your average dog or human. Our bodies are designed to wash away heat with efficiency, and perhaps that's why I didn't wither to a crisp in the intense heat. But I knew I would if I stayed down here much longer.

I was on a kind of beach which stretched out to my left and right. Behind me the ground rose sharply to a precipice. A narrow path led up there, over a ledge towards a smouldering mountain range. At the top of this, three volcanoes spewed ash and magma into the sky and earth.

I wasn't sure it would be any cooler up there, but I had to take my chances. I took one step, and a massive roar erupted from the sky. Up there, I saw a familiar creature – a demon dragon just like the one I'd defeated in the First Dimension. If it noticed me, I was doomed.

Well, I guess I was doomed anyway – I was in the Seventh Dimension after all.

I made my way across the rocks, keeping my feet as light as possible so I didn't tear my paws on the jagged rocks. I crept away from the boiling lake, and it quietened a little as I progressed. A hot wind came off the boiling sea as I climbed, but it didn't feel like it would kill me anymore. Still, it was hot enough to be uncomfortable; hot enough for me to regret hating the snow.

The passageway up was narrow, and the rockface shot up almost vertically on my right. I hugged this as closely as possible. The earth seemed to sap some heat away from me, and I tried to keep as far away from the lava as I could. Eventually, this wall gave way, forcing me to navigate across a terrifying ridge. I know I'm a cat, and I know I'm excellent at keeping my balance. But the ground underfoot pierced my feet with each step I took, and part of me wanted to just give up and tumble off the side.

Still, I persevered, and I eventually climbed up to a plateau where I could tread a little more readily. The ground was too sharp for lying down, much as my body wanted to do so. But the plateau stretched out far enough to shield me from the heat from below. I knew I needed water, desperately, and I was also ravenously hungry. I hadn't eaten since those sausages last night when fire had actually felt good.

I sniffed the ground for a sign of something, but all I could smell was the sulphur from the molten earth. I tried to detect some movement using my whiskers. But the earth was rumbling so much that I couldn't sense anything. Still, I could see, and I could see well. Something scurried across my path in the distance, and I entered a low crouch to stalk it.

It wasn't long until I recognised the creature from the way it moved. A demon rat – I had hunted many of these before in Astravar's abode. It didn't seem to notice me stalking it, with the roaring coming from the lava below and the rumbling of the earth. But just at the last moment, I readied myself to pounce, and it twitched its nose, turned towards me and scurried off.

I followed it at a pace, knowing that though it wouldn't provide much nutritional value, it would ease my hunger pangs somewhat. It led me over the rough terrain, under a few nefarious looking archways made of craggy rock, and then towards a lake – this time much higher up than the sea – full of smouldering water.

Before I could catch it, it disappeared in a hole in the rock-face. I tried to reach in to fish the demon rat out, but the rock scratched my foreleg, and I yelped out in pain. That was when I sensed something behind me. I don't know if I heard it swishing out of the water, felt its gaze upon me, or sensed the heat coming from the cracks in its skin.

I turned, worried about what beast I could face. Could it be a demon dragon? A demon Maine Coon? A demon chimera? None of these, I admittedly wanted to have to face again, especially in their own realm.

But what I saw before me was much, much, worse. The bulbous and fiery eyes. The huge nostrils that vented steam just like Salanraja's. The buck teeth...

It turned out that I was standing face to face with a demon hippopotamus.

33

AMMIT'S SERVANT

The demon hippopotamus was the largest land creature I'd ever seen. Actually, I tell a lie; it didn't quite dwarf the forest golem that I'd battled in the forest back in the land I wished I was back in. But it was larger than the demon Maine Coon, larger than any size Ta'ra had ever grown to, perhaps even as large as an elephant. Well, in all honesty, I'd never seen an elephant, but I'd heard stories about them from the Savannah Cats back home, how they had legs as big as tree trunks that could pancake a cat before it saw what was coming.

This demon hippopotamus had a nose as big as a tree stump, and a head made of sharp grey rock that looked like it could hammer me into the ground. Just like any demon creature I'd seen, it had cracks all over its craggy skin, fire brimming beneath them.

Behind it, the volcanic lake bubbled and boiled, and raged out sulphur into the air. I wondered if there were more demon hippos lying in wait for me there. Maybe they had all sent this one ahead to drag me back into its pond where they could boil me in it until my flesh became tender.

I could only imagine what fate lay in wait for me, but I didn't want to hang around long enough to discover it either. The demon hippopotamus opened its mouth and out came a sound like a thousand pigs playing the trombone. It sent the hackles up on my back. With a dry mouth and my heart pounding against my chest, I turned to flee.

The beast scuffed the ground behind me, and the rock beneath me shuddered and creaked. Hot air rushed towards me. I shrieked and dived out of the way as the massive creature came crashing past. It skidded to a halt, sending up plumes of ash around it.

I backed away, this time realising that I needed to watch the demon hippo carefully to survive this encounter. It turned slowly, snorting and grunting like no pig I'd ever heard before.

I tried shouting out at it in the demon language. "Demon Hippopotamus, I command you to return to your lake."

But it might have been deaf, or it might have been too stupid to understand me, or maybe in fact it didn't even speak the demon language or any language for that matter.

I tried again. "DEMON HIPPOPOTAMUS. I COMMAND YOU TO LEAVE ME ALONE."

At that, the demon hippopotamus snorted out a laugh. "I OBEY ONLY AMMIT, THE DEVOURER, THE GREAT BRINGER OF DEATH, THE EATER OF HEARTS. YOU CANNOT COMMAND ME."

That didn't sound good, and I groaned, anticipating what might come next. The demon hippo lifted itself up on its stubby legs, kicked the dust up behind it, let out its snorting, bellowing roar and charged at me again.

This time, knowing it was faster than me, I didn't turn my back to it. Rather, I watched in terror as it sped towards me with its buck teeth raised over its wide gaping maw, ready to swallow me whole.

I steeled myself, no matter how much my legs wanted to flee. I measured the distance between that massive gaping mouth as it drew ever closer. I waited until I could see the fires burning at the back of its throat, behind the shadow of a massive tonsil that looked like a bell. The beast had breath that smelled like a salami fished out of the sewers, which made me want to retch. Still, I didn't dare run, at least not yet.

Before it could devour me whole, I ducked to the side, and I leapt onto its back, just as I had with the demon dragon. I thought I might be safer there, but when I saw it was charging right towards that boiling lake, I dived back off again.

The demon skidded to a halt just before the lake. As it turned, I looked around for a way to escape. I could retreat to the ridge, but in the distance, I could see the demon dragon I'd previously seen overhead had perched itself there. The plateau stretched out in most directions for quite a way until it vanished into a shroud of smoke. At one point, the ground rose into a wall of smoothed volcanic rock, jet black save for a slight shine to it, reflecting the red glow from the lava below.

The demon hippopotamus' eyes burned even brighter than before, but this time it didn't charge. Instead, it ambled up towards me, and I had no choice but to back up against that obsidian wall.

I hadn't noticed it before because of the angles, but one side of the wall jutted out in front of the other. This created a corridor wide enough for both me and the hippo to pass through.

I took the chance, and sprinted through the passageway, and found myself on an outcrop of rock, surrounded by a steep drop into the churning lava sea. I felt queasy looking down at it, and I could taste the acrid fumes at the back of my mouth.

The demon hippopotamus emerged from the passageway at its slow, steady pace. "YOU WILL BE A PRIZE FOR MISTRESS AMMIT. SHE WILL BE PLEASED WITH ME, OH SHE WILL. YOUR HEART SMELLS GOOD, AND I CAN HEAR THE WAY IT

BEATS. SO CLEARLY NOW. THE MOST BEAUTIFUL HEART I'VE HEARD FOR A WHILE."

I yelped. I had nowhere to go. The demon had me blocked off completely. My only choice was to jump. I turned away from the hippo and readied myself to leap into the lava sea.

This was the end...

"It is not over yet, young Ben." A voice said in my head, smooth with a lilting Welsh-like accent.

The crystal...

"Have courage, and do not give up until your very last breath."

My crystal... But how was it speaking to me here in the Seventh Dimension?

"Your destiny doesn't lie in the jaws of a demon hippopotamus. Come, this way."

Suddenly, the air in front of me shimmered. Well, actually it was shimmering quite a bit already given the intense heat, but let's just say that it shimmered even more. It also sparkled a little, with a golden sheen, as if made of fairy dust.

The patterns the light played in the air revealed a spiral staircase leading up, with no railings on either side of it. It didn't have any substance, and it looked like my body would pass right through it. But I could feel the furious breath of the hippopotamus so close now. In moments, I'd be toasting within its mouth, and moments later it would deliver me to its mistress Ammit, whoever that was.

"Have courage, Ben. Courage will keep you safe."

I guess I had no choice – if I stepped on this staircase and plummeted into the fires of the earth, it would make no difference. I would have died anyway.

I took the first step, and when I felt it was solid enough underfoot, I dashed up a few steps. The infernal creature beneath me also tested the staircase with its hefty foot, but it couldn't step onto it and almost fell off the cliff. It backed off just in time, which was a shame because I'd wanted to see it fall. The beast made another one of those mighty pig trombone noises – almost loud enough to knock me off through sound alone.

I braced myself and followed the staircase up to wherever it would lead.

34

THE SAME CRYSTAL

The magical staircase led into a dark chamber with three walls, a floor, and a ceiling formed completely of obsidian. It was slightly cooler in here – if that was at all possible in this place – and it would have been completely dark if it weren't for the white light emanating from a giant-size crystal I knew so well. It spun slowly on its vertical axis, showing depictions of me in flight on Salanraja's head with a staff in my mouth, which let off a beam of red energy.

My beam shot out and met a beam of purple energy head on. Alongside me, Astravar flew astride a bone dragon, his staff emitting that second deadly beam which he clearly wanted to kill me with. The crystal had shown me this scene many times, in different variations. It knew many possible threads of the future, but they all seemed to lead towards this ultimate battle between me and Astravar.

The thing the crystal never told me is who would actually win.

It's impossible, I thought. I had to be hallucinating because of the heat. My crystal couldn't possibly be here when it was in the First Dimension, right in Salanraja's chamber where we had left it.

"*What is it about my existence that you fail to comprehend?*" the crystal – or should I say my hallucination of the crystal – asked me inside my mind.

"*You're not here. You cannot be.*"

"*And you do not understand magic well, Ben, for you have slept through your classes. It exists across the dimensions, as does each crystal, including the one you see now.*"

I took a moment to take that in. Really, my head was spinning so much, and I wanted to faint. No water. No food for hours. Heat exhaustion. I just couldn't think straight. "*Hang on a minute,*" I said after the third time I'd considered the crystal's words. "*Are you telling me you're exactly the same crystal as the one in the First Dimension?*"

"*That's exactly what I'm saying. I exist across all seven dimensions.*"

"*Then it was you who saved me from the demon hippopotamus just before it was about to eat me. Whiskers, why did you wait so long?*"

"*No,*" my crystal said. "*You saved yourself. I merely provided the tools for you to do so, but you took the leap of faith necessary to survive. That, young Ben, is the lesson you must learn. When and when not to leap.*"

As the crystal bathed me in its cooling light, I became less and less fatigued. I still felt so terribly thirsty that I would drink even the foulest reeking swamp water, and my stomach rumbled like an earthquake. But my clarity of mind at least returned to me. I looked over my shoulder at the raging volcanic tempest below, and I wondered if I would have to return to it.

"*Can you get me out of here?*" I asked.

"*Perhaps,*" the crystal said. "*If you deem yourself worthy.*"

"*What do you mean?*"

"*You have already proven yourself ready. The time, Ben, is nigh.*"

"*For what?*"

"*Your second test. You can now gain your second ability. That is, if you have the strength to do so.*"

"*I thought you said I couldn't gain it until I battled the chimera and won?*"

"*That's right,*" the crystal said.

"*But I can't fight the chimera. It was bad enough to face the demon Maine Coon when it was just that. But then Astravar turned it into a demon chimera. I don't have a chance against that.*"

The crystal let out a soft noise that sounded like wind chimes trying to sigh. "*It isn't the chimera without that you must defeat, Ben. It's the chimera within.*"

"*The chimera within? What nonsense is this?*"

"*Are you ready for it?*"

"*I—*"

"*Are you ready, Ben?*"

I hesitated. I guess, in all honesty, I didn't have a choice. It was either fight the chimera within – whatever that meant – get eaten by a demon hippopotamus or be consumed by the Seventh Dimension's boiling sea.

"*Fine, I'm ready.*"

"*Very well...*" A cooling breeze washed out from the crystal, reminding me of those times the master or mistress would open the boxy freezing machine on a hot day. On the breeze came a scent of lavender that pushed the sulphurous fumes away. As the wind came, the crystal spun faster and faster. The light intensified from it, and the crystal soon was moving so fast that it appeared round.

"*Close your eyes, Ben,*" the lilting voice of the crystal said. "*It's time to face the chimera within.*"

I didn't even think twice about disobeying it. The words mesmerized me, and my eyelids felt heavy. They closed on their own accord, and I felt a pressure against my eyelids, soft and not in the least bit painful.

My thoughts became random; my mind became wild. Soon enough, the crystal had woven its spell, transporting me into my world within.

THE CHIMERA WITHIN

The crystal dropped me from the scorching heat of the Seventh Dimension into the scorching heat of a desert in the noonday sun, and I didn't appreciate that one bit. The ground was so hot that I had to keep moving so my paws didn't burn. I was thirsty; I was hungry; I knew that if I didn't find what I needed soon, I'd collapse here and die.

But this was all in my imagination, surely? But then maybe my sensations were those of my body in the Seventh Dimension. Maybe the heat and the fumes there were getting to my head. Maybe everything I'd just seen – the crystal, the magical staircase up to the obsidian chamber, the demon hippopotamus – were all hallucinations.

Still, I could physically feel the heat in my paws, and I didn't want to linger long enough to test my theory. I trudged across the sand, lethargy burning in my legs, my tongue as dry as a cactus, my vision hazy, as I tried to see through the bright light reflecting off the sand. There were no plants, no vultures, not even the smell of anything living. A flat, desolate plain of yellow stretched out in all directions, rising to darker dunes behind the distant haze.

"*Believe, Ben,*" the crystal said in my mind. "*Believe and you shall find.*"

Well, if it was going to be like that, I thought I might as well imagine what I wanted, and I wanted water the most of all. I thought of that lake near the invisible Faerini city, where Ta'ra and I had lapped up water. I thought of the moat at Dragonsbond Academy where the water tasted faintly of roses, and where I would often visit for a sneaky drink. I thought of my home in Wales on those days that it rained – admittedly half the year – and how I could step outside after the downpour and drink the water from a puddle.

Low and behold, I spotted a shimmer on the distant ground – closer to me than the horizon. Water, it had to be water. I picked up the pace, bounding towards it at a sprint, forgetting that I should really conserve energy in this heat.

Luckily for me, it wasn't a mirage, and I soon found myself in a glorious oasis with one of the clearest lakes I'd ever seen. I cowered under the shade of a lonely palm tree, and I lapped up the smooth water until I could drink no longer. Then, I tracked the minnows darting around underneath the lake's surface, as I tried to devise a way to fish them out. But I didn't need to, because I suddenly smelled smoked salmon. A meal of it had presented itself in bite-sized chunks in a bowl right at the base of the palm tree.

I mewled in happiness, entirely convinced that I had died and gone straight to cat heaven. Maybe here, bowls of my favourite foods grew on trees and appeared when I most wanted to eat them. I devoured the salmon in what must have been minutes, and then I turned back to the lake, licking my lips.

It finally seemed a good time to have a nap, so I lay down in the sand, appreciating the coolness where the shade covered me from the beating sun. Just as I closed my eyes, a bellowing roar filled my surroundings, accompanied by a terrible stench.

The Savannah Cats back home had told me so many times that the lion's breath smells nastier than rotten salami. When I could finally return home, I looked forwards to telling them that the chimera's breath is ten times worse.

My eyelids shot open, and I spun around to see the lion head's open maw right in front of me. This wasn't the demon chimera, but the same chimera I'd seen in my dream, days ago in Driar Brigel's alteration class. A hissing sound, then the snake's head whipped around the chimera's body, lunging right at me. I dived out of the way just in time. Then, as I bounded away, the goat let out that hideous, ear-piercing bleating noise.

I ran back into the desert, not caring so much now about the scorching earth. Rather, I wanted to get as far away from that beast as possible. I'd had enough dealings with nasty things that could tear me apart for one day. I just wanted a peaceful life. I wanted to go back home.

Salanraja, I said in my mind, wondering if I could reach her. *Salanraja, I need help.*

But there was no answer. Whatever dimension I was in, she wasn't here now. Instead, I was sprinting right towards a form as splendid as a lion, silhouetted against the sun. It had the tail of a snake and horns sticking out of a head from its back.

I stopped in my tracks and checked over my shoulder. How had it found its way around me so fast?

As the beast scuffed its hind hoof against the ground, kicking back the sand in a cloud, I spun around again and sprinted, putting my entire back into it to give me as much speed as I could.

But I realised I was just sprinting towards the sun now getting low and red in the sky. And there was the chimera standing in front of me again.

This isn't real, I told myself. *This is just a dream.*

"*The experience isn't real,*" the crystal said back in my mind. "*But your emotions are, and so are the ways you've trained yourself to react to them. It doesn't matter which world you're in, Ben. You must learn to circumvent instinct.*"

While the crystal spoke in my head, I continued to sprint towards the chimera. My body hadn't quite registered that it wasn't running away from the previous chimera. But I stopped myself in my tracks, just before I reached it.

Then I turned to run again.

"*Is this what you want, Ben?*" the crystal asked. "*To be constantly trapped in a spiral of fear?*"

"I want to go home." I replied in my mind. "*I want life to be easy again.*"

"*So, take responsibility for your emotions and measure your actions against them. Then, maybe, you'll eventually discover a way.*"

Whiskers, the crystal was right. I couldn't keep running like this. I had to turn around and face the beast. It was only a product of my imagination after all. It couldn't surely kill me, could it?

I stilled my thoughts, and I stopped my body, and I refused to listen to that part of me that said, 'run'. I turned slowly and stared into the brilliant yellow eyes of the beast. It was only a couple of spine-spans away from me, and I could smell its revolting breath in the warm air.

I held that gaze, and for a moment time seemed to stop between me and the chimera. The snake's head might have hissed, but it remained poised above the lion's head as if charmed. The goat's head also glared at me from a little to the side of the chimera, as if measuring what I would do next.

You have to fight the chimera, the crystal had said to me.

I lowered myself into a crouch. The chimera did the same as if it was my reflection. I hunched myself over my forepaws and the chimera mirrored my very motion. I opened my mouth and let out a hiss. The chimera responded with a tremendous roar.

The thought came to me for a split second to turn and flee. But I pushed it away. I let the beast's roar and its breath wash over me. The snake's head raised itself, as if also poised ready to strike. The goat's head lowered its horns behind the lion's head.

I don't know where I got the strength to do what I did next. It went against every essence of my being. But I let my muscles follow through the same motion I would when hunting a mouse. I leaped into the air, and the chimera also launched itself off its haunches. I readied my paw to swipe at its head, also seeing five sharp extended claws arcing towards me. I kept my eyes open, even though part of me thought I would die.

A sudden coolness washed over my body as I passed right through the chimera as if I'd passed through a waterfall. The sun flared bright white in front of me, and then a wave of calm washed over me.

I turned once more, ready to continue the fight. But the chimera was much more distant from me than it should have been. It didn't look menacing anymore, instead sitting on the sand regarding me. It gave me a humble bow, and then it ran off into the distance, leaving me alone on the cooling sand as the sun plummeted down towards the horizon.

I turned to see that I'd magically been transported back to the oasis. Darkness descended in the sky behind the lake, but the water was still lit by my crystal which emanated a soft and warm white light while spinning suspended in the in air.

"*That was it?*" I asked in my mind. "*I thought I had to actually fight it and win.*"

"*You did win, Ben,*" the crystal said in its beautiful lilting Welsh accent. "*You did what you needed to do. You defeated the chimera within.*"

"*But we didn't even touch each other. It wasn't even there.*"

"*It was there. It's always been there within you and will be until you draw your last breath. You've just never learned how to confront it until now.*"

"*Well, it was easier than I thought,*" I said, and I realised I had my head raised high. I'd regained my normal cat-like stance, standing the way that I'd always stood around my neighbourhood in South Wales.

"*What is easy? Surely you can only do what is in your control.*"

"*You might be right...*" I looked up at the sky, which was clear and now full of twinkling stars. "*So, I guess it's time for my second ability.*"

"*It is...*"

"*What do you have in store for me this time? Will you give me my staff, perhaps?*"

"*You're not ready to wield your staff yet.*"

"*But I defeated the chimera.*"

"*Still, you have many lessons to learn.*"

The crystal started to spin, and I felt an intense pressure on my eyelids. It felt as if someone was sticking two knitting needles into the skin there, but I knew better than to back away. My body felt warm, and my muscles convulsed as they took on a new form. I mewled up to the sky, and then I suddenly felt my face twist, and I roared. My tail hissed back at me, and I could swear that my shoulder blades became horns as my spine bleated.

Then my body went back to normal. Yet my muscles felt stretched, as if I'd been doing that funny human activity called Yoga.

"*What the whiskers was that?*"

"*You now have your second ability,*" the crystal said. "*Congratulations.*"

"*But what is it? I can transform?*"

"*Now, you can bring the chimera within, without. But be careful,*"

Ben. Alteration magic is powerful and if you transform into it too much you will become just like the chimera within – feral and soulless."

I thought about Astravar's threats about transforming me into a feral beast. *"I will be careful."*

"Good." Shimmers of gold appeared on the surface of the lake, and the crystal vanished. Instead, just below it appeared a white portal. It was so bright I couldn't determine where it led. *"Step through, Ben."*

"Can this take me back home?" I asked, hope flaring up in my chest.

"It will take you where you need to go. Now make haste, before the chance is lost."

I didn't question the crystal's motives anymore. As long as it didn't take me back to the Seventh Dimension, with the demon hippopotamus waiting to drag me underneath the boiling waters to its mistress, then I would be better off.

I sprinted right across the solid magical surface overlaying the lake, and through the portal, a chill washing over me as if I'd just passed through an incredibly icy and powerful cascade.

36

REJOINING THE TEAM

The crystal's portal took me to where I'd entered the Faerie Realm originally – the clearing where we'd tried to stop Astravar from entering the Second Dimension with his demon chimera and his crystal. It was the place where we'd taken down a load of Manipulators, and fought against a forest golem. I hadn't known what the outcome of the entire battle had been until now.

It was night, and it was absolutely freezing – particularly after having spent the last hours being toasted by lava and then crossing the scorching midday desert floor. But a campfire roared out from a little way away, and I gravitated towards it, letting the heat wash through my fur.

"Well, look what the cat dragged in," a familiar voice said from behind the fire once I reached it. It belonged to Initiate Rine, who peered around the fire, his chin lit red by the flames. All my friends who had travelled with me to the Willowed Woods sat there, save for Ta'ra. I paid them no heed. Rather, I scanned the ground for anything that could wet my tongue and stave off the thirst. I found a puddle of melted snow just by the campfire, and I lapped up the entire thing in several gulps.

As I drank, Aleam, Ange, Rine, Asinda, and Lars all fired a barrage of questions at me. Ange even stood up and walked over to me and stroked me at the back of the neck. But I needed to rehydrate myself before I dealt with trivialities, and so I sought out more puddles and drank to my heart's content. As I did, Seramina glared at me from her seat, in her usual disturbing fashion. Prefect Asinda also watched me with a suspicious frown.

"*Bengie,*" Salanraja said in my mind, and then she roared out from the sky. "*You've returned. What happened? I was so worried about you! I couldn't sense you anywhere.*"

I looked up to see her shadow pass overhead. The dragons weren't nearby, which meant they were probably on some kind of mission. As she spoke to me, the dragon riders stopped asking me questions, as if they knew instinctively I was about to have a conversation with Salanraja.

"*I went on a little adventure,*" I said.

"*I know that. But you just jumped right into the Second Dimension. You should have waited. We thought Astravar would kill you.*"

"*Well, he didn't. Although he almost did...*"

"*Why, what happened?*"

"*He sent me to the Seventh Dimension, and then I had to escape from the boiling lava, and I almost got eaten by a demon hippopotamus, but I got away.*"

Salanraja let out a mighty laugh in my mind. "*Ben, that's impossible. You must be pulling my little dragon foreleg.*"

"*It's true!*"

"*Then how did you get out? There's no way to return from that place unless someone opens a portal from another world.*"

"*Our crystal... I found a version of it in the Seventh Dimension,*" *and it made me battle a chimera, then it told me I could turn into a chimera, and then it sent me back here even though I asked it kindly to send me home."*

Salanraja hesitated a moment. I felt annoyance rise within her.

"There you go again," she said.

"What?"

"All you seem to ever think about is food and going home. Does our bond mean nothing to you Bengie?"

"Well, I'm sorry, but I didn't choose to come into this world."

"Suit yourself. But if I'm not important to you, I've got some scouting to do." She flew off and I didn't hear from her for a while.

Ange stood there with her hands on her hips, staring at me. But it wasn't an angry stare. She probably understood that I wanted to talk to my dragon first. Everyone here would understand, really. We were all dragon riders, after all.

Instead of having a civil conversation with my dragon, I'd just come back into this world for Salanraja to complain about my attitude. I would have thought she'd be telling me what a hero I was, and showing a little sympathy for me, and actually explaining to me why the ability to turn into a chimera might be useful.

But no! She'd had to give me a massive guilt trip instead.

Did all dragons treat their riders that way?

I stalked up to Ange and mewled, hoping for a little comfort. I rubbed against her leg, but I still felt a little tender and so I ended up groaning instead.

"Ready to speak now?" Ange asked.

"I think so," I said.

"Then come and tell us all about your adventures," she turned back towards the logs that Driar Aleam, the three Initiates, and the two prefects sat on. They had more sausages on sticks toasting over the campfire.

I jumped up next to Aleam, and mewled, purring. He looked down at me. "I guess you're starving," he said, and he tossed me a sausage from a bag. I devoured it gleefully. I might have had smoked salmon only minutes ago, but I'd only eaten it in my imagination and my stomach knew that.

Aleam tossed me a second sausage, and then a third, and I didn't feel good until I was halfway through that one. Then, I licked my lips, and I sat down and told my story.

When I got to the bit about becoming a demon chimera, everyone there seemed kind of shocked. They looked between themselves, and Seramina stood up and loomed over me. She glared down at me with those burning eyes, and I sensed something rummaging around in my mind, as random thoughts went through it. I hid behind Aleam's back so she wouldn't be able to do what she was planning.

"Did I say something wrong?" I asked from my hiding place.

"No, no," Aleam replied, and I could feel his voice vibrating through his back. "Initiate Seramina, I don't think there is any cause for worry." He shifted over, so Seramina could see me again. She was still glaring, but not as intensely I guess, or at least I didn't have that probing sensation anymore.

"Okay, so what's this about? I would have thought you'd all be happy to see me."

"We are," Ange said. "Believe us, we are. It's just..."

"What?"

Aleam placed his hand over my back and stroked down my fur. "You're different, Ben," he said. "We all know that."

"Of course, I'm different, I'm a cat."

"But you use two kinds of magic," Ange said, her mouth agape.

"What?"

Aleam stood up, and he drew some patterns in the dirt with his staff.

"For a long time, no one since dragons and humans bonded, has been able to use more than one kind of magic. When you gained the ability to speak multiple languages, I thought your crystal had chosen you for mind magic. But now you also know alteration magic. We're all just a little surprised, as many of us were equally surprised when we discovered Seramina could use both mind magic and clairvoyance magic."

"But didn't you say that you were a dark magic user once?" I asked Aleam. "So you'd have been able to use lots of different types of magic, just like Astravar."

Aleam shook his head and took a deep breath. "I sacrificed that ability when I found my crystal and bonded with Olan. I lost my abilities, but I also lost the risk that dark magic would eventually consume my soul."

He stared into the flames a moment, as if remembering, and we all shared a moment of silence.

"So, what does this all mean?" Prefect Asinda broke the silence, standing up. She stood next to Seramina and gave me an almost equally unnerving glare. "It could be the crystal Astravar nestled inside him. Maybe it's corrupting him, pushing him towards the dark."

Prefect Lars stood up, took a place next to Asinda and held her hand. He looked down at me for a second, shook his head. "Sorry, Asinda, I can't believe that. Ben has helped us too many times. Surely, we must accept the rules are different now. I mean, no crystal has chosen a cat before as a magic user."

"Exactly..." Ange walked over to me and tickled me under the chin. "I couldn't believe that little Ben here could become an evil warlock. Could you, Ben?"

Rine snorted, and then he spat out some water, angering the flames of the fire.

Asinda turned her harsh gaze on him, then she spun it around on Ange. "Must I remind you, Initiate Ange, that I'm a prefect here, and you should show me some respect."

Ange turned away from her. "Sorry," she muttered under her breath, and she looked down at me. I rolled over on my back, and I let her tickle my tummy for a moment. Then, when it got a little too uncomfortable, I gently pawed her hand away.

"I think Prefect Lars is right," Aleam said, with his hand on his chin. "We have to accept things are a little different with Ben. Not only is he a cat, but he's also from another world. His crystal has already predicted things we'd never even have dreamed of."

"But what if his abilities make the cat turn evil," Asinda said. "What do we do then?"

High Prefect Lars squeezed her hand, and I wasn't sure if it was to encourage her against speaking out of place, or to communicate his support. Really, I thought having Bellari as an enemy was bad enough. But to know that Prefect Asinda wasn't on my side was worrying. With Driar Yila as her auntie, she already knew people in high places.

I wanted to open my mouth and point out that I'd helped save her. And as for Ange, it was she who used her leaf magic to break them out of their prison. She should be grateful for this, and I was just about to tell her so. But before I could get in a word, Aleam cut in.

"I'm sorry, but we have more pressing issues," he said, and he looked up towards the sky.

"What is it, Driar Aleam?" High Prefect Lars asked.

"I've just heard from Olan, and he's spotted Astravar."

"Astravar?" I asked. "Did he leave the Second Dimension?"

"He has his army of Cat Sidhe with him," Aleam said. "Much as your crystal foretold."

"Then we must stop him at once," I said.

"Yes, we must," Aleam said. "Everyone, call back your dragons at once from their scouting locations."

Though I didn't really feel like talking to Salanraja, I thought I would rather go with them than stay in the Willowed Woods alone, where a forest golem could smash me to smithereens. I reached out to call Salanraja back to our location.

Then we all listened as Aleam told us the plan.

37

THE PLAN

R ine, Ange, Lars, and Asinda beat out the fire with nearby branches as they also turned an ear to what Aleam had to say. This sapped the heat out of the surroundings and the wind that buffeted through the willows was icy and cut to the bone. I never thought I'd say this, but it actually felt good to have a little chill in the air after coming back from the Seventh Dimension. In the distance, I heard the howls and gnashes of wargs. But they didn't seem to dare come anywhere near us magic users – which I guess was a wise choice.

In a way, listening to the beasts, I wanted to turn into a chimera, run out and teach them all a lesson. But I remembered what the crystal had told me about not using the ability too much, and so I decided it was better not to.

The Initiates and prefects had heard it before, but Aleam said he wanted to check they completely understood their roles. Aleam also explained, for my purpose only, how Prefect Lars would use his shield magic to create a shield, while Aleam, Rine, Asinda, and Ange would use their elemental magic to help give that shield strength.

Their goal was to protect Seramina in a protective force field, as she used concentrated mind magic to reverse the spell Astravar had cast on the crystal. The crystal had not only converted the fairies to Cat Sidhe but had also taken control of their minds. So long as it brimmed with power, every single Cat Sidhe in Astravar's army would be completely under his thrall.

"I still don't get it," I said. "Why do we need to do this reinforcing stuff? With lightning, ice, fire, and leaf magic, surely we have enough power to defeat Astravar."

Aleam shook his head. "Dark magic is a truly wild thing. It has a mind of its own. The warlocks weren't mad at the beginning, but prolonged use of this ruthless magic caused them to lose their minds.

"Astravar has gone so far down that path, that he now has enough power to destroy an unfortified magical barrier, powerful though Lars' shield magic is. If we leave ourselves undefended, we'll open ourselves up for attack from his minions, and the most important thing is for us to guard Seramina so she can take Astravar's crystal down."

"And your elemental magic can make the shield stronger?"

"Now you're getting the hang of it," Aleam said. "It's not actually the warlock we're dealing with, but the magic that has taken over his mind. We need to work as a dedicated team to defeat it. But I'm sure Driar Yila has explained this in classes, Ben. It's first-grade stuff."

I yawned as I thought of Driar Yila trying to explain things. I could swear she spent more time telling people off for things than actually teaching anything valuable. It was always the most trivial things that bothered her, like students drumming their fingers on their table, creaking their chairs against the floor, and sleeping in class.

"I forgot," I said, and I thought I'd better leave it at that.

Aleam rubbed his chin. "I'm sure you did..."

I tried to ignore his lack of confidence in me. "So, after this," I said, instead, "Seramina will break the crystal's magic, and the dragons will fight whatever Astravar throws at us. But we won't hurt the Cat Sidhe, will we? We won't hurt Be'las, and Go'na, and Ta'ra?"

"Not unless we have to," Rine said.

I glared at him. "And what's that meant to mean?"

"It means that we'll do everything in our power to keep the Cat Sidhe safe," Ange said. "That's one of our oaths in Dragonsbond Academy – to protect non-magical life from those that seek to destroy it."

"I hope that doesn't mean we have to become vegetarian..."

Ange laughed. "I didn't mean it like that..."

A roar cut apart the sky, and Salanraja swept down to land. She'd been the closest to us, given she'd only just gone on scouting duty when I'd come through the portal. Given dragons could only communicate long distances without a rider, Olan had thought it better if she kept watch before I arrived.

She still didn't speak to me though, and that suited me just fine. I was tired and had enough information about magic running around my mind that it was making my head hurt. Seramina sat on the log, right next to the ashes of the fire. She glared at me like always. I remembered what Aleam had said about having to accept people even if they seemed a little odd, and so I decided I should try to connect to Seramina.

So, I went over to her, letting her heady snowdrop perfume wash over me. I sat next to her. For a while, she sat there stock still. Then, she surprised me by reaching out with a soft hand and stroking me gently on the back of the head. I purred – she felt better than I thought she would. Her hand was actually warm.

"I came over," I said, "to check that the Cat Sidhe are going to be in expert hands. Are you up to the task, Seramina? Because I'd do it myself, if I could use magic like yours. Is my friend, Ta'ra, going to be safe?"

"She's more than a friend to you," Seramina said.

"And what's that meant to mean?"

"I mean only what I read. Astravar's destiny isn't the only one intertwined with yours. Ta'ra's is too, as well as my own. The four of us are interconnected, I just wish I knew how."

Aleam turned to Seramina and looked at her with a slight expression of alarm on his face. I don't think she noticed but I did, and I made a mental note to ask the old man about it later.

"You really are odd," I said, as I pushed my nose into her hand.

"That's what people tell me," Seramina said. "But what do you expect of a girl who can manipulate minds and read destinies?"

"But aren't you scared? Because I would be if I were you. You have all that responsibility, and you have to stop Astravar destroying the city."

For the first time, Seramina looked away. "I'm absolutely terrified. But I still need to do it, because this is what my crystal has foretold."

I mewled and rolled over on my back, and she reached over to rub me with a delicate touch. "So, what exactly has your destiny told you?"

Seramina retracted her hand. "That's personal. No one should ask of the destiny of a seer."

"I'm just curious," I said, and I jumped down from the log to watch the other five dragons that flew towards us in a v-formation. Salanraja moved out of the way, to give them plenty of space to land.

"Well," Aleam said, as he dusted off his hands. "I guess it's time to be off then."

"Just one more thing," I shouted back. "You all have roles, but what should I do?"

"Stay out of trouble," Asinda said. "And keep within Lars' shield."

"Yes, ma'am," I said. Really, I was beginning to think she was more bossy than her Auntie Yila. Anyway, maybe I'd find a way to be useful. I had after all gained a new ability, and part of me was itching to try it out.

38

FLIGHT TO BATTLE

Salanraja took off into the sky first, and she wasn't gentle about it. She beat me against her corridor of spikes as she whirled around three times in the air. Really, I'd mastered flying so long as it was gentle, but I hadn't yet toughened my stomach for such extreme aerobatics.

"Salanraja, what did I tell you about grace while flying?" I asked.

"I just thought I'd start knocking some sense into you... Literally."

I found it hard to get my thoughts together with me tumbling around and around on Salanraja's back. The way she was going, I thought she was planning to toss me right off her, and then I wondered if she was going to catch me again. Maybe, she'd decided that I wasn't useful to her anymore and her life had been so much better before she'd found me.

I waited until she took a break from spinning around, and had entered a glide, before I told her what I thought she wanted to hear. Beside me, I heard Rine crying out in pleasure as Ishtkar did a half loop-the-loop, followed by a half barrel roll in the air.

"*Fine,*" I said. "*I missed you when I was in the Second Dimension.*"

Salanraja crooned from underneath my feet. "*Do you mean that?*" she asked.

"*No... I'm just saying it, because I don't want your bad flying to cause me to throw up.*"

"*You know,*" Salanraja said. "*I quite enjoy 'flying badly'. Besides, Rine seems to enjoy it, so why don't you?*"

"*Because I don't have a sadd—*"

I didn't have time to finish my thought before she did it again. She entered a corkscrew motion towards the ground, rolling over and over. All I could see was the world spinning below, and it looked for a moment like we were going to crash into the trees. Round and round I went, banging against Salanraja's spikes.

"*Stop, Salanraja!*"

She levelled out at my command. "*Do you have something to say?*"

"*I can't take this right now. I went through quite a bit of torment in the Second Dimension, you know. Not to mention what happened in the Seventh Dimension after that.*"

"*Fine,*" Salanraja said, and she pushed herself back up in the air to join the other dragons who had now entered a flying formation. Olan once again was at the front – Aleam looking again like he was moulded into the saddle. The wind whipped against my fur, and I rushed up to Salanraja's head, appreciating the sensation of it.

"*This is much better. Now let's fly along pleasantly like this, shall we? We can worry about the fancy stunts if we encounter any of Astravar's bone dragons.*"

Salanraja laughed into the sky from underneath me. She shook her head a little as she did, but this time she was gentle enough not to risk throwing me off my perch. "*I really missed you, Bengie. When you went into the Faerie Realm... I don't know, it's hard to* describe. *It's as if someone tore a piece of me right off my flesh and took it away forever. As if I'd lost a wing or something.*"

Strangely, I hadn't felt the same. But then I'd been so worried about Ta'ra, that I'd not really had time to.

"*We've not always been together,*" I pointed out. "*We did quite well before we met, don't you think?*"

"*But didn't you always feel that something was missing?*"

"*I've never even thought about it. Though now I do, I was quite happy in my world, until Astravar brought me over here.*"

"*Didn't you feel somehow incomplete?*"

"*No... Did you?*"

Salanraja let out a low and pronounced growl, and for a moment I thought she was about to start her bad-flying antics again. But she no longer seemed to have the energy for that, thankfully. "*I wasn't happy before. They said that they'd either have to cut off my spikes or they would force me to be a passenger dragon for King Garmin and his court. I didn't think I had a way out of it, until I found the crystal...*"

"*What crystal?*"

"*It doesn't matter... I shouldn't have said anything.*"

But cogs were beginning to whirr in my head. "*The crystal?*" I asked. Then it dawned on me. "*You mean our crystal?*"

"*I...*"

"*Salanraja, are you telling me that you knew about our crystal all along?*"

Salanraja shook her head slightly, and I held on with my claws to stop myself sliding off.

"*It wasn't until you entered the dimension,*" she said. "*Olan, Aleam, and I stopped Astravar from destroying it. We couldn't believe it at first. But it showed what you were capable of. It showed that you could defeat Astravar and help to save our kingdom.*"

"*So, you mean that when you met me for the first time, you knew that you were going to bond with me. Why then were you so angry and cruel to me? And why did you almost roast me alive when I was just hungry?"* I didn't know how to feel, really. Salanraja had been lying to me all this time.

"What was I meant to say? Hello, you are destined to bond with me and defeat an evil warlock. You would have run away and never come back."

Now, it was me that was growling. *"You could have been a bit nicer to me at the start. There was no need to torture me in your corridor of spikes like you've just done. Admit it Salanraja, you just want to be in control of everything around you. You want to control me."*

"That's not true at all," Salanraja said.

"Then why did you try to scare me when you first met me?"

"Because you weren't the hero I hoped you'd be," Salanraja said, *"and I thought you needed to learn a few lessons in humility."*

"Is there anything wrong with being proud of my heritage?"

"Not if you behave the way your ancestors might have," Salanraja said. *"But it's not just about the food. I could sense that you put on a big show to hide how afraid you were of this world, and I wanted to help teach you how to handle it. How to exhibit true confidence in a situation you know nothing about."*

Part of me wanted to complain more. But then, I remembered how horrible it had been in Astravar's tower when he'd had me trapped there many days ago. I remembered how Salanraja had heard me when I was in trouble and saved me from getting eaten by a spider and its army of serkets. I remembered how she had hunted out so many delicious meals for me to eat.

"Thank you... I do appreciate you Salanraja. Though I wish you'd told me right from the start what I was getting myself into."

"It doesn't matter now, I guess," Salanraja said.

"I guess not..."

My ears twisted towards a sound coming from the distance. Crows. Thousands of them, cawing against the cold swishing wind. *"Do you hear that?"*

"Yes," she said, and it appears that we weren't the only ones who did, because from the centre of our formation, Olan cried out. Together, the dragons joined in the chorus, including Salanraja who tossed her head around as she roared. I scurried back down her neck into the protection of her second ribcage.

Aleam pointed with his staff at a glimmering object on the horizon. I could just make out a faint purple mist rising up around it, and as we got closer, I saw it to be Astravar's purple crystal.

The cawing from the crows intensified, and they scattered in a wide cloud. A cacophony of screeching roars then overtook the cawing, and a dozen bone dragons shot up into the sky. They barrelled towards us, but Olan was already leading our small squadron towards the ground. We swept down so fast, that we got right underneath the bone dragons.

We approached a thicket at the edge of the forest. Salanraja crashed through and touched down lightly. I couldn't see where the other dragons landed – all I could see was purple mist and the dust and leaves that the dragons had whipped up from the ground.

I sprinted down Salanraja's tail, then I looked out for the first Manipulator. It had its white staff pointed up at a bone dragon, leaching energy through the thick canopy through which I could ever so faintly make out the bone dragon wheeling around above. Salanraja took off to pursue the bone dragon, whilst I bounded towards the Manipulator.

I knew how to defeat it now, and I could see the glimmer where its crystal was. Without thinking, I leaped towards the wraith-like formation of spectral light. I took its crystal in my jaws, and then I scurried as fast as I could away from the creation, the crystal's magic burning in my mouth.

From a little way to my left, an ice bolt shot out and hit another Manipulator. To my right, I could see the forest writhing as well, as if being manipulated by leaf magic. Both Rine and Ange were therefore nearby.

Red light flared from overhead, and then a bone dragon came crashing down and shattered into parts when it hit the ground. I dropped the crystal to the floor, satisfied. *"Congratulations, Bengie,"* Salanraja said in my mind. *"Looks like we got the first takedown."*

"I guess we make a good team," I said.

Thunder cracked, then I heard the roar of fire shooting out from nearby. I smelled something charring, then lightning flashed from the sky. Soon after, came a sound like shattering glass, and the smoke in the air mixed with the smell of ozone. Two more bone dragons crashed down through the canopy.

Rine then came rushing towards me. At first, I thought he was pleased to see me. But then, I saw a Manipulator chasing after him. It was sweeping down its spectral staff in a slow arc, and I knew it would only be a matter of time before it fried my friend with its magic.

I put all my strength into my legs, and I rushed towards the ethereal creature. By the time I was upon it, its staff had started to glow, still pointed at Rine. I leaped in and took another crystal in my jaws. I carried it a safe distance away and deposited it on the ground. Then I turned around, and Rine bowed to me as if to say thank you.

Two more bone dragons came crashing through the forest, and I had to dive out of the way of one of them so as not to get crushed. I peered through the dust that the bone dragon had sent up into the air, to see Aleam pushing through the thicket, brushing off his hands. Prefect Lars charged in from the side and Aleam shouted out, "Everyone to me!"

Behind Aleam, a bright purple light pushed through the tree-

line. I guessed Astravar stood beyond that purple light, and he probably had his army of Cat Sidhe with him, including Ta'ra.

I didn't waste a moment. I bounded up to Aleam, and Rine,
Asinda, Ange and Seramina quickly joined us. Once we were in
place, Prefect Lars raised his staff to the air, and out shot a fountain
of white light. This rose to a central point and then dispersed
around us to form a large dome.

It made a terrible buzzing noise – as if we'd just discovered a
beehive. I flattened my ears as much as I could to ward off the
sound, and that was enough to at least concentrate on what was
happening.

Staring at the shield was even more mesmerizing than watching
birds through the window. It had a hypnotic effect on the eyes – the
way that it sparkled and glowed. The magic seemed to pass over the
shield, producing an effect much like rain washing over glass.
Honestly, the way it looked, I didn't think it would hold anything
out. It looked like even a mouse could pass through it, much like
one passes through a waterfall.

I tested the shield by rubbing my nose against it. It let off this
electrical stinging sensation, and I immediately backed away. It was
definitely solid.

"Everyone ready?" Aleam asked.

Everyone gave their affirmatives.

"Right," Aleam said. "Charge!"

39

THE SHIELD

Though it was a charge, we didn't move particularly fast. We might have done if we didn't have Aleam within the shield. But he was an old man, and he wasn't on his dragon. So, we moved more at his hobbling pace. Prefect Lars also seemed to be moving incredibly slowly as he concentrated on feeding energy into this shield barrier that was meant to protect us. The dragons hovered above us, tracking us as we went.

"Now," Aleam said as we walked. "This is your first team shield. Remember what we talked about. I'll provide the energy first. Then, Asinda, Rine, and Ange you're to fuel the lightning with your elemental magic. Are we ready?"

"Yes, Driar Aleam," Asinda, Rine, and Ange said together.

"Good," Aleam said, and he pointed his staff towards the top of the shield. A yellow beam came out of the crystal at the top of his staff and met with Prefect Lars' beam. The air around me bristled with static, causing my fur to stand on end. Meanwhile, the shield wall took on a yellow hue.

Asinda, Rine, and Ange already had their staffs ready, and they also cast beams of red, blue, and green towards where Aleam's and Lars' beams met. The air around me tamed a little, and the shield took on many more colours, a spectrum washing across it as if someone had taken a rainbow and poured it all over this shield.

It was hot in here, and my mouth felt dry, so I stopped to take another drink of water as we passed a puddle on the ground. But I only managed to get a mouthful down before the shield wall caught up with me. It brushed against my fur, and then I felt a sensation in my side like a sharp static shock ten times magnified. I yelped and scurried away from the shield, and then decided to keep as close to Prefect Lars as possible.

Seramina had her staff poised, and her fiery eyes tracked the purple crystal as we approached it. A smell of fear accompanied her scent of snowdrop perfume, and so I mewled and rubbed against her leg to give her a bit of support. I thought it would be one way to be helpful so that she didn't mess up her task of destroying the crystal and saving Ta'ra.

It must have taken us a good five minutes of this slow hiking, to arrive on the scene. Astravar had set himself up in a hollow, bereft of plant life. But I wasn't sure if this was a natural phenomenon, or if he'd scorched the place with his magic for convenience. That same horrible stench rose from the ground, as always. Fortunately, though, I couldn't smell it now, and so it didn't affect my breathing. The crystal kept the mist out, and I could only smell everyone's sweat, Seramina's, Ange's, and Asinda's perfume, and a thick atmosphere of ozone.

It turned out that the crystal wasn't the only source of light here, but Astravar still had the portal open. Cat Sidhe were flooding out of it, coming out in groups of three, each the size of a panther. There must have been thousands of them, lined up in neat rows like cat soldiers and they were all staring at a point behind the crystal. Well, I say staring, but I was sure that their eyelids were sealed shut.

The lines cut off in the centre to form a circular space, maybe a hundred spine-spans wide. Astravar stood at the centre of this, his long cloak flapping in a wind we couldn't feel behind this shield barrier. The demon chimera stood next to him, grooming itself with its three heads. Fortunately, none of them were faced towards us.

The warlock had his back turned to us, and so he didn't seem to see us or the dragons approaching. Really, that surprised me as this shield was making such a racket that, even with my ears almost fully flattened, I could hardly hear myself think. Added to which, the combination of us and the dragons would have been incredibly easy to spot. Astravar's magic must have required intense concentration, which was probably why he would have sent those Manipulators and bone dragons to deal with us – so we wouldn't interrupt him.

Masses of purple crystals lay on the floor around Astravar and the chimera – no order to how they were arranged. They fed thin streams of light into the crystal on Astravar's staff, which he had raised high. This let out another beam towards the massive dark magic crystal that hovered overhead, much as it had in the fairy's throne room just before he'd banished me to the Seventh Dimension.

"What's he doing?" I asked Aleam.

Aleam was concentrating so much that his reply was slow. "He's charging the purple crystal. Presumably, the more power he can feed into it, the more powerful he'll be when he attacks Cimlean."

"*If* he attacks Cimlean ..."

"He will."

"How do you know?"

"Because it's only ten miles in that direction," Aleam said, nodding towards where Astravar and the Cat Sidhe all faced. "Now shush. We need to focus. Seramina, are you ready?"

"Yes, sir," Seramina said, and she lowered her head and tightened her grip on her staff.

Aleam narrowed his eyes, and then looked up as if to double check the shield was sound. "Okay, let's do this," he said.

Seramina nodded, then took a deep breath. I moved in front of her.

"I'm here for you, Seramina," I said. "You can do this." I also gave her a nice, cute meow, to tell her that I really believed in her.

For the first time ever, I saw her smile. It was only for a moment then, immediately after, the lines on her face tightened and her jaw clenched. Her eyes, I could swear, flared bright red and a white beam erupted from her staff. It hit the crystal head on where it blossomed into a wide spot.

That was when Astravar finally noticed our presence. He pivoted around his staff, slowly, and though he was still quite far away his stare felt like he was right here looking at me. He opened his mouth as if to call something out, but with this incessant buzzing I didn't hear what he said.

It was as if an army of statues suddenly sprung to life. The Cat Sidhe all stood up as one, and they stalked towards us. They surrounded us with their fangs bared and their eyelids shut, and a few of them tested the shield with their paws. But their attempts to affect the shield bounded off it. I looked out for Ta'ra – remembering the mark I'd scratched on her cheek. I couldn't find her though.

In front of us, Astravar hunched his shoulders while he twisted his staff slightly. The flow of energy from the crystal to Astravar's staff reversed. Now, both the crystals on the floor and the massive dark crystal fed his staff, which he swung down towards us.

The beam swung with it, and it hit our shield straight on.

Prefect Lars grimaced, and clutched his staff with his second hand, his knuckles whitening. Everyone else took on equally contorted expressions, as the light from their staffs brightened even more.

"Keep it strong," Aleam said. "We can defeat him."

I wanted to do something too, but I felt absolutely powerless. So, I arched my back and hissed at the Cat Sidhe that circled around the shield to communicate that if they did find a way in, then they'd have me to deal with. Behind them all, the crystal had reddened around Seramina's beam, and this red was slowly spreading out across the crystal. It was only a matter of time before she destroyed the thing.

Meanwhile, Astravar seemed to realise that he wouldn't break the shield through his magic alone. So, he decided to change strategy, and his beam of magic switched from purple to blue.

The energy from his beam spilled out over the shield, forming swirling patterns that merged and coalesced into a roughly round shape. The shield buzzed even louder, but another sound started to take its place.

Astravar cackled like he had all the time in my dreams. It wasn't long until we could see his eggshell-skinned face, projected onto the shield, looking down on us with those lifeless grey eyes.

I shrieked, and then I hid behind Aleam. But this time, it wasn't me he had come to talk to. Instead, he went straight to the source...

He seemed to want to talk to Seramina.

🕸 40 🕸

DISRUPTED

"There you are, girl," the face of Astravar boomed from the shield wall. "At first I thought you were a mere mind-witch. But when I saw your magic, I knew you were something special. Now, I see why. I guess you've always wanted to know who you are."

Aleam turned over his shoulder and looked at her with an expression of alarm. "Remember what we talked about, Seramina. Whatever he says, you can't listen to him. You can't trust anything he says."

"Ah, Aleam," Astravar said, and he had to shout to make himself heard over the roar. "Always the old deceiver. When did you all plan to tell the girl the truth? Seramina, all that time in the orphanage, did you ever wonder why you were there? You lost your mother, but whatever happened to your father?"

"What's he talking about?" Seramina said.

"It doesn't matter for now," Aleam said. "We need to focus on the task at hand."

"Oh, and then what will you do?" Astravar asked. "Kill me? Really, Seramina, do you want to kill your own father?"

Seramina's eyes tightened, and the light went out from them. Her beam lost some of its energy, but she still kept it focused on the point. "You're lying... You can't be..."

"Of course he's lying," I said, and I went back over to her mewling and rubbed against her leg. "Astravar isn't to be trusted. He's a bad man, and he hurts people and cats... Focus, Seramina. Ta'ra's life depends on it."

She didn't seem to be listening to me though. Her eyes flared bright red again, and she turned her fiery gaze on Aleam. "Driar Aleam, what is this about? Is he my father?"

Aleam lowered his head. "I didn't think he would have a chance to talk to you."

"Just tell me the truth," she said through clenched teeth. Her hands were shaking, and I wondered if she was about to drop that staff.

"Seramina, whatever Astravar was, he isn't now. Now, the magic has consumed him. Please, thousands of lives depend on you breaking the magic in that crystal. You can't let him get to you."

Asinda walked over to Seramina and put her hand on her shoulder. "It's okay..." she said.

"Don't touch me," Seramina said, and Asinda backed off. Seramina cut off the white beam coming out of her staff, and she dropped the staff by her side.

"See, that's it..." Astravar said. "Let me do my job, and we'll get this underway. Maybe you'll later want to join me, daughter. Your magic is powerful, and I think you'll make a fine warlock."

But Seramina was shaking her head, tears brimming in her eyes. "Mother dying young, then all that time in the orphanage. Having to fend for myself. She never told me who my father was... No one did!"

"I was always going to come back for you," Astravar said. "Once I gained dominion over this world, there was no way I would let your life go to waste. Not with so much power inside of you."

"No!" Seramina shouted, and she raised her staff again. "I can't let you do this. I don't care who you are, but I grew up in Cimlean. You'll destroy everyone I ever loved."

"Did you really love them?" Astravar said. "The magic coursing within you. Why do you think you're so powerful? And you have destiny magic, I see. So, you already know our fates are intertwined. That magic – all your magic – I gave you a birthright. No one else alive has had such power since birth."

"No!" Seramina shouted again. "You've been corrupted. You might have once been my father, but you're not anymore." A flood of energy came back out of her staff. The crystal took on the same redness as before.

"Seramina, stop!" Aleam said. "You're pushing it too far."

His voice was soon drowned out by Astravar's maniacal laugher. "That's it, my daughter. Let the anger fuel you. Now if I only open a channel between us, I wonder what I might find."

The energy beam coming from her staff intensified, and it took on a slight purple hue. Seramina writhed about on the spot a little, and her face twisted. Her eyes burned ever more brightly, and her brows were furrowed as if in concentration.

"So much power, in there," Astravar said. "So much darkness. You never realized the potential. Now, all you need to do is sleep."

"Don't listen, Seramina," Aleam said. "Control your mind."

But Astravar hummed a deep and sonorous tune, and he managed it so loudly now that I didn't think Seramina could hear Aleam's protests. "Sleep, my darling," Astravar sang between hums. "Worry not about the light. In the darkness there is grace. Fear not my darling. From your fear you can escape."

His song was kind of mesmerizing – so much so that it almost sent me to sleep.

Seramina narrowed her eyes. "I don't care who you are. Just get out of my mind!" The air started to heat up around her, and it was as if a whirlwind erupted within the shield. It buffeted around her, and then I noticed the fire had left her eyes, and instead I could only see the whites of them, glowing with a purple sheen.

That was when the beam from her staff became a deep purple. Her magic lashed over the shield, causing it to crackle, as if someone had just thrown fireworks at it. The shield flickered, and its intensity faded.

"Astravar's possessed her," Aleam shouted. "Somebody do something."

Rine cut off his energy beam, and he edged towards Seramina. He didn't get far before another beam came out of her staff and threw him backwards.

"That's it, daughter," Astravar said, and he cackled maniacally. "Feel the power. You have my blood and can become just as powerful as me. A servant to my cause."

More beams came out of the staff, this time tentacles meant for Prefect Lars. They whipped against his feet and tripped him up. The shield fizzled out.

Above us, the dragons roared, and they went in to attack.

"*Be careful,*" I called out to Salanraja in my mind.

She didn't say anything back, and I know what she would have said anyway. If she'd had a chance, she would have told me that fighting Astravar was much more important than her life. Much more important than the bond between us that she held so precious.

But the dragons didn't go far, because Seramina had a massive ball of purple magic glowing above her staff as the whirlwind whipped around her. It drew energy off the massive crystal hovering above Astravar, who had already mounted his demon chimera as if ready to flee.

The ball left Seramina's staff and shot upwards towards where the dragons had gathered. It exploded into one massive shockwave that sent all of them tumbling down from the sky. They crashed into the floor, at such speed that they looked like they must have broken bones.

As they fell, Seramina also fainted to the ground.

"Salanraja!" I screamed out loud. The other dragon riders also called out their dragons' names, and then all fell silent. With my heart thumping in my chest, I thought that our lives would be over then. Astravar would command his army of Cat Sidhe to devour us, and I'd probably get eaten by Ta'ra given how that evil warlock seemed to love irony.

But Astravar didn't seem to want to waste time, and he put two fingers in his mouth and whistled. The Cat Sidhe, who still surrounded us, growling, suddenly jerked upright and turned to face Astravar. Another whistle, and they were off, with Astravar leading them from his mount on the demon chimera, the crystal keeping pace above him.

For a moment, I watched after the Cat Sidhe army, sprinting soullessly after the purple crystal.

"Ta'ra!" I shouted. "Ta'ra…"

I had to stop her. I had to do something.

But I couldn't face them alone. They'd eat me alive. So, instead, I bounded over to Salanraja to check if she was okay.

41

COUNCIL BRIEFING

I made a sad mewl when I saw Salanraja lying there on the ground, so helpless. I mean, I'd seen her sleeping, but then I could feel the fire burning in her belly as I slept next to her.

Now, there was no fire inside her. Aleam had told us the dragons weren't dead. But Seramina or Astravar had cast some kind of coma spell on them, and he didn't think they would wake up anytime soon.

I felt guilty. Salanraja had worried about me so much when I'd entered the Faerie Realm. Then, when I'd come back, she'd told me that my departure from this world had torn her apart. Meanwhile, I hadn't even considered Salanraja in the second dimension. I'd thought a lot about Ta'ra, while Salanraja hadn't even crossed my mind.

Now, I could feel that sense of emptiness inside me that Salanraja spoke of. It was as she'd described it – as if a part of me had been ripped away. Like losing my claws, perhaps, or my ears.

Aleam had found some spiky plant that looked a bit like aloe in my world, except with longer spines. He had broken this apart to access the sap inside, and he was walking around administering this to the other dragon riders, who rubbed it into the chest area near their dragon's hearts.

Only Seramina wasn't at work, and that was because she had passed out. She now lay with her head propped up by her charcoal dragon's, Hallinar's, wing. The spell that she'd cast, Aleam had explained, had absolutely exhausted her.

Aleam had already tended to Olan and Hallinar, and now he came over to Salanraja and placed some salve on her body. It was green, sticky-looking, and smelled like the desert. I moved over to help rub it in.

"Best I do that," Aleam said.

"What, why?" I really wanted to feel helpful here.

"Because you will take half of the sap back away on your fur, and right now it's Salanraja that needs healing."

"Will she wake up?" I asked. "Is that what the salve is for?"

Aleam put his hand to his chin. "We can't apply anything to break the spell. But the salve will help the blood flow more readily."

"But when she wakes up, will she be all right? She took quite a fall. They all did. Maybe they broke some bones."

"Don't worry," Aleam said with a dry chuckle. "Dragons actually have quite a malleable bone structure, which comes as part of their magical make up. They can survive falls from incredible heights, and so yes, I'm sure once the dragons wake up then they'll be flying right back over to us."

"And when will they wake up?"

"It could be a matter of minutes, or it could be a matter of days. There's no way of knowing."

"Whiskers," I said. Meanwhile, we'd let Astravar march on Cimlean, and we had no dragons we could use to catch up with them. Olan had told Aleam that she'd sent out a call for reinforcements telepathically to Dragonsbond Academy when she'd discovered Astravar. But it would take them hours to get here, and Astravar would reach the city in an hour, if that. Of course, they also had a good twenty dragons in the city to stand guard. But with what Astravar had at his disposal, Aleam had told me we'd need all the dragons we had.

I was interrupted from my reverie by Seramina letting out a groan as she stirred. I walked up to her as she opened her eyes. She reached out, as if trying to find her staff. But Aleam had placed it in Hallinar's panniers for safekeeping.

Seramina stood up sharply and then moved towards Hallinar.

"Don't you move an inch," Prefect Asinda said, and she stormed over to Seramina and pointed her staff at her. "We need to know first whether you're safe. Who do you serve, Initiate Seramina?"

Ange strolled over to join Asinda. "With all due respect, Prefect Asinda, you can't just burn her with your magic. She's human, and she's probably on our side."

"Oh yeah," Asinda said, and raised her eyebrow at Ange. "Then you do something."

"Fine," Ange said, and turned to Seramina. "Sorry, but this is for everyone's safety." She pointed her staff at the ground. The leaves there stirred, and tree roots broke the soil. They grew quickly, tangling around Seramina's ankles.

Just as Asinda had instructed, Seramina didn't move an inch.

I walked up to her and sniffed her feet, and then I pushed my nose under the hem of her trousers, so I could sniff her skin as well. "She's fine," I said to Ange. "You can release her."

I looked up to her, and she glanced across at Asinda, who glared daggers at me. "You're not to listen to the cat, Initiate. What are you now, Ben? A diviner?"

"No," I said. "I can smell people's emotions."

"And is that some kind of dark magic too?"

"All cats can. Because when you feel things, you release chemicals into the air. And I can tell you that Seramina's scared, and she's stressed, and she feels embarrassed and you have nothing to fear."

Aleam sighed, and then he stood up and walked over to Seramina. He gently took hold of her chin and gazed into her eyes.

"She's fine... You can release her, Initiate Ange."

Ange nodded and pointed her staff at the ground again to loosen the roots' grip on Seramina's ankles. But it didn't seem to matter whether or not she had the bonds, because Seramina remained standing in the same place, her posture as rigid as a broomstick.

"You can move now, Seramina," Aleam said.

Seramina's posture melted. She turned to the old man. I walked around her to keep track of what she was doing with that stare. But her eyes had lost their fire, as if the tears streaming out of them had doused the flames.

"He took control of my mind. I'm sorry. I was weak, and he was so strong in there. I shouldn't have let it happen. I shouldn't have lost control."

Aleam gave Seramina a sympathetic look. "It's easier to beat yourself up about a bad experience than to learn from it. But that doesn't mean it's the best thing to do."

"But he used me. He didn't care about finally meeting his daughter. He just wanted to use my feelings about it to control me. And I let him..."

Aleam lowered his head. "We shouldn't have kept it secret from you. If you'd been prepared for it, he might not have been able to exploit it."

Seramina shuddered, and then she wiped away the tears with the back of her hands. Then she clenched her jaw. "This time, I won't let him get to me. I'll use my magic, and I'll destroy that crystal, and I'll show that warlock how strong I am."

"But how will we get there?" Aleam said, looking over his

shoulder at Olan. "We've got no choice but to wait until the other dragons arrive, and by then I fear it will be too late."

"There is another way," I said. I stepped back into the spot where Astravar had previously stood underneath the crystal, and I mustered the power inside me.

Rine, having seen the commotion, had sauntered up over to stand next to Ange. Now, as he watched me, his eyes went wide. "You have to be kidding," he said, obviously understanding what I was getting at. "We ride dragons, not cats, and certainly not chimeras."

But Prefect Asinda seemed concerned for a completely different reason than pride. "Stop that!" She pointed her staff at me, its crystal glowing red and fire brimming at the front of it. "We don't need any more dark magic."

Lars stepped forward, and he pushed down her staff with his hand. "His crystal gave him that magic," he said. "And I think we should trust its judgement. It has everyone's best interest at heart."

Asinda let out a long sigh. "Fine..." she said, and she lowered her staff.

I waited a moment to see if anyone else had any intent of frying me. Satisfied all the dragon riders were now on my side, I began the transformation process.

When the crystal had told me I'd have the ability to turn into a chimera, it had never told me how painful it would actually be. My skin writhed underneath my fur, and my muscles bunched up, making me feel like my entire body would tear apart. My tendons tightened, an enormous lump grew out from my back, and my tail hardened with scales.

At the beginning the pain caused me to yelp and groan, but by the end of it, I was letting out what I imagined to be terrifying roars into the sky. Another part of me bleated, and I felt suddenly as if I had a second mind to use just like my first. Then there came this hissing noise from my tail, and I turned to see a snake poised right above my rear.

Except, it was strange, because I also had the mind of this snake, and I could shift my vision to see my head looking back, as well as my goat's head bleating out in pain. It all looked a little blurry through the snake's eyes, but I could also feel the temperature of everything around me in its glands. I could sense the heat emanating off the dragons and the dragon riders. I could see little mice and voles scurrying through the forest. I could see faint traces of things moving everywhere around me, from the birds in the sky to the earthworms wrestling underneath the soil.

My vision through the goat's head was a little less interesting. Through its eyes I could see normally, except without the colour red. But then, to make up for it, I could see virtually in all directions, as if I had eyes in the back of my head.

Really, I'd never considered how other animals saw before, but now I understood why the old Ragamuffin from back home said to avoid long grass because you never know when an adder is going to strike. With this kind of heat sensing capability, even a cat wouldn't stand a chance in the dark. The old Ragamuffin had also advised that if we ever saw anything with horns – be it a bull or a goat – then the first things we should do was run.

This was why, I guess, Salanraja had always told me to fear the chimera.

"Well," I said. "I hope I'm massive enough, because I feel strong enough to carry you."

Aleam laughed. "You're much bigger than I expected. Big enough for all of us, in fact."

"So, I guess everyone should hop on." Through the senses of all three heads, I could tell clearly where the Cat Sidhe had gone, especially as I smelled their pheromones in the air using my super-sensitive snake tongue – because, weirdly, snakes smell with their tongues and not their noses.

Ange, with her hands folded beneath her waist, looked back nervously at Quarl. "What about the dragons? We can't just leave them behind."

"I'm afraid we have little choice," Aleam said. "Besides, nothing's going to do anything to a dragon, sleeping or not."

"True that," Ange said, and she stepped forward.

"Then what are we waiting for?" I said. "Let's go and defeat Astravar."

Without further hesitation, the dragon riders mounted me. Seramina sat at the front, so she could have a direct view of the crystal in case she needed to attack it in flight. Prefect Lars sat behind her, then Asinda, then Aleam, then Ange, then Rine at the back. I thought they'd all be heavy. But honestly, this chimera transformation must have included super-strength, because I hardly noticed their weight.

"Ready?" I called.

Everyone murmured their consent, and I bounded off over the plains leading to Cimlean, following a scent that I'd come to know all too well.

42

CIMLEAN CITY

I don't know how long it took me to reach Cimlean, but I'm sure it took much less time than I'd thought it would. I used to think that I was fast as a Bengal. But now, with these goat's legs to power my rear and give me a spring to my steps, and my lion paws to keep me stable, I covered the ground faster than I'd ever known. I probably went even faster than the Cat Sidhe.

I stopped on a rise around a mile before the city so we could assess the battlefield. The city looked just as the crystal had shown me in the vision of it getting destroyed. The white walls contrasted against the surrounding snow, giving the whole place an impression of innocence. The golden towers shone out from behind the walls, and archers stood looking out from upon the walls. They had their bows raised waiting, it seemed, for the Cat Sidhe to charge.

These Cat Sidhe sat below, still panther-sized, staring at the city as if awaiting orders from their master who stood at their centre, his demon chimera by his side. Like before, he had a massive circle cleared around him, with the crystal hovering overhead to give him room to cast his magic.

I wondered if the Cat Sidhe could grow large enough to knock down the walls and cause carnage throughout the city. If they could do that here, they could do it anywhere. Who'd have thought that the death of humans wouldn't be caused by famine or plague, but by massive rampaging cats?

Although it wouldn't be caused even by that because we were going to stop him.

Astravar already had his crystals ready from his pouch. He threw these into the air, and purple sparks from the overhead crystal gave them energy. They lit up like comets, and they charged towards the archers. I only saw them ever so faintly, but I knew what was going to happen next.

The magical crystals would burrow themselves in the archers' foreheads. Then, the archers would become possessed by the crystals, much like the Cat Sidhe had. They'd turn their bows on the city, and light their arrows, setting their own houses aflame. Once carnage had been wreaked, the Cat Sidhe would charge in, and the city would soon be Astravar's to claim as his own domain.

I had hoped that the warlock wouldn't have made it this far. But his conquest had already started. Which meant we had to move fast.

"This is it then," I said loud enough for everyone on my back to hear.

"It sure looks like it," Aleam said. I couldn't see him through my cat's eyes, but I could see the back of his head through my snake's eyes. "Everyone dismount, then Lars get the shield ready."

"Should I turn back into a cat?" I asked. One thing I remembered from Driar Brigel's lesson on alteration magic was that if I stayed in any form long enough, then I risked becoming it. Though this chimera had its uses, I didn't want to take it as a permanent form. Honestly, I felt like the other two heads were cramping my style – particularly the one of the goat.

"You should probably hold this for a while, Ben," Aleam replied. "A chimera might have its uses."

"Like what?" I asked. "We'll be inside the shield."

"I don't know," Aleam said. "But I'm sure Astravar has more tricks up his sleeve."

I growled, not so much because I was angry but because it felt good to growl with a lion's voice. High Prefect Lars raised his staff and called out for us to join him. We all gathered together, and Lars cast the shield, which buzzed like a thousand bees all around us. Then Ange, Rine, Asinda, and Aleam cast their elemental magic to strengthen the shield. Meanwhile, Seramina kept her staff ready. I could smell fear in her, but I could also smell anger, and I could see in her expression that she really didn't want to mess this up. The air once again took on that magical scent of ozone.

It took us a good five minutes to get close enough to the crystal for Seramina to do any damage. The crystal hovered in the air, with Astravar standing underneath it. The Cat Sidhe surrounded him in an obedient circle. This time Astravar wasn't casting any magic, and he saw us approach.

He decided this time not to project his face on the sphere. But rather, he spoke out in my mind. Usually, I guess Seramina would have done something to keep him out of there. But she had her eyes focused on the crystal as she readied her staff.

"*Dragoncat,*" he said. "*How fitting. You've gained your second ability. Now, I see you're a chimera.*"

"*Astravar,*" I replied. "*We won't let you take the city.*"

"*Oh, how quaint. It looks like you've learned the virtues of team-work. But don't you think a team's much better when they're all under your command?*"

"*I think not. They're better when they feed you and look after you and comfort you when you're feeling down.*"

Astravar cackled out in my mind. "*You're still the same old cat.*

How you can even consider that you can defeat me with such a ridiculous attitude, I don't know."

"I'm not going to defeat you this time..." I waited for a moment until the mind magic beam erupted out Seramina's staff and hit the crystal dead centre. *"Seramina is."*

"Hah, I didn't think she'd come back for another pass. I guess she's strong – she has my blood after all."

"You're not strong. You're weak and you're a coward."

"Really? How so?"

"Because you let the dark magic consume you when you could have fought back against it. Now, you're destroying the world, even though there's part of you inside that should try to reconcile with your daughter. You never had the courage to fight the dark magic inside you. Seramina does, though. And, so do I!"

"Oh yeah," Astravar said. *"Well, maybe I am a coward. But, you know, there's one thing about cowards. They're much better at surviving than heroic fools. Now, dragoncat, I've had enough of your meddling. I thought you'd make a useful minion one day, but I've decided you're better off dead."*

By this point, fissures had spread out across the faces of the crystal, and it looked like it would break apart. If Seramina could rip the thing into pieces, then the spell on the Cat Sidhe would be lifted. All I had to do was keep Astravar talking.

But he wasn't stupid, and he already had plans of his own. He pointed his staff at us and out of it came a purple beam that hit the shield dead on at around knee height. At the same time, his demon chimera tossed its head upwards and let out a roar. I didn't hear it from this side of the shield, with the constant buzzing and humming noises that grated in my ears. But I could feel the anger in it, all the same.

A sudden flash of light spread out around the impact point on the shield. This cloned itself on our side of the shield. The centre of the light evaporated, to create a kind of halo, looking as if Astravar had cut a hole right out of the shield. The sound around us cut off, and time seemed to distort. A sudden cutting breeze washed in through the shield, and I shuddered as it brushed over my skin.

Through that hole, I saw the demon chimera bounding towards us.

43

CLASHING HORNS

"What in the Seventh Dimension?" Aleam said. "A double portal."

"A what?" I asked.

"No time to explain. Brace yourself, Ben. Astravar can only hold the spell for a moment."

I growled, my eyes fixed on the red smouldering eyes of the demon chimera's lion's head. It growled as well as it leapt through the double portal which closed behind it, sealing it in. The demon chimera's eyes weren't on me but Seramina, and it charged towards her. But I moved to block its path. It rammed into me and we tumbled across to the other side of the shield dome.

For a moment, I saw Seramina's tiny shoes, and I thought we'd trip her up. But she side-stepped out of the way just in time.

"Seramina, keep it steady," Aleam said. "Ben will take care of this."

Too right I would. I had the demon chimera pinned down with my paws on its shoulders. It roared at me, and its nauseous, sulphurous breath washed over me. I bit down towards its neck, but it clawed at my face, causing a painful gash that felt like three iron pokers hitting me at the same time.

My goat's head was bleating, and my snake's head was hissing. Meanwhile, I roared out in pain as well, just as the demon chimera threw me off it. I tumbled across the ground, sending up dirt and dust.

The demon chimera picked itself up again, and it approached Seramina more slowly this time, its snake head raised in the air. She didn't seem to notice it there, but Aleam swung down his staff and sent a bolt of lightning at it. But this didn't seem to harm the beast much. Naturally, I guess – I remembered from my lessons that demons could only be slowed and not harmed by magic.

"I've almost got it," Seramina said. "I just need one more minute."

But she wouldn't have that minute, as I could already see the demon chimera's snake head lurching towards her. I didn't waste a moment. I charged right at it and caught the snake's head in my jaws. I overshot a little and ended up pulling the demon chimera along the ground with me. I grunted as I hit the shield wall, stinging my face. I released my grip, and the demon chimera's snake bit me on the side of my rump. It felt like being stung by a large wasp. I guess I was too massive a beast for the venom to affect me like it had before. Despite that, if I took enough lashes from that thing, it would probably kill me.

Outside the shield, the king's dragons had risen from the city, and they were flying towards Astravar. Astravar and his army of converted archers were now fighting back against the dragons, and so they kept high in the air – probably unsure what to do. A flash of panic shot through me as I thought they might attack the Cat Sidhe army. They might kill Ta'ra. Fortunately, though, Astravar's magic was keeping them at bay.

In front of them, the crystal's fissures now ran deep. White light fizzled underneath the cracks, and the whole thing looked like it would erupt within moments. But if the demon chimera took down Seramina, then I didn't doubt Astravar would win.

It was then that I noticed there weren't as many Cat Sidhe amongst Astravar's ranks as before. Instead, I noticed gold specks glistening in the sky. Whiskers, Astravar was about to send fairies out to sacrifice their lives and bring the king's dragons down. They'd explode, and die, and Ta'ra could be amongst them. But I couldn't do anything but fight the chimera and hope Seramina would break the crystal soon.

Meanwhile, the demon chimera had circled around to face me. It had realised, I guess, that there was no getting to Seramina without going through me first. We circled each other, growling, our gazes locked on each other. The buzzing of the shield seemed to get even louder, and then I saw what the thing was doing. It was trying to back me into the shield so it would fry me. It would be a quick death – I guess – electrocuted, burned, frozen, and warped from the magic that Aleam, Asinda, Rine, and Ange cast against the shield.

But then, I realised it was only a matter of timing. I stopped myself still, facing the demon chimera head on, making myself a target. It seemed to accept the challenge, and it scuffed its back hooves in the ground, and charged, lowering its goat's head, ready to ram me into the shield. I counted to three, then I lowered my goat's head and our horns locked.

The demon chimera had the momentum, and it pushed me back a little, sending my rear into the shield. It burned there, and I felt the intense pain where the chimera's snake had bitten me before. The snake on my tail hissed, and for a moment the pain was so intense that I thought I might as well give up. My snake's vision, my goat vision, and my lion's vision all went hazy, and I was just about ready to quit and die.

This was a demon I was facing, after all. It was far too strong.

"You must defeat the chimera..."

The crystal's voice, I heard it in my head then.

"Not the chimera without, the chimera within."

Suddenly, I realised what it was talking about. Astravar had given up when he'd lost the battle against dark magic and succumbed to it. But Aleam had been a hero and kept his will strong. I also needed to be the hero, because though I faced off against a demon, my chimera was a creation of magic. I only needed to will the strength and I would find it.

I roared from my lion's head, tucked underneath my chest. Meanwhile, my goat's head shrieked, and my snake's tail lashed out. I willed strength into my rear hoofs, and I used my front lion's paws to keep purchase against the ground. I pushed with all my strength, and after a couple of inches, I was free of the shield.

Then, inch by inch, I pushed the demon chimera back. And I continued to push, and though my nemesis struggled against me, it didn't have enough will within it to hold on. I mustered more strength within, imagining myself as a stampede of goats charging at the demon chimera. It bleated, and it growled, and hissed as I backed it into the shield. I pushed it even further until I could smell smouldering rock and the sulphurous fires of the earth.

Soon enough, the beast collapsed on the ground, and the fires underneath its cracks went out.

A bright white light then flared out from in front of the city. This faded, to show the crystal shattering into pieces, shards of it scattering in every direction. Some of these hit the shield, sending up blue sparks on the outside.

The Cat Sidhe remaining on the ground immediately came to life, and they surrounded Astravar with their lips bared in fearsome snarls. They closed in on him and they looked ready to tear the warlock to shreds and eat him for lunch. It was ironic really, given that the fairies had been vegetarians in their own kingdom.

In response, the warlock raised his staff to the sky and a flash of bright purple light shot out of it. This faded, leaving a trail of purple mist surrounding a clump of snow, and a crow flying away towards a large flock awaiting it in the distance.

44

THE CURE

P refect Lars lowered the shield, and I transformed back into a Bengal, not wanting to listen to the ingratiating hissing of the snake, and the ear-piercing bleating any longer. I'd decided by this point that the three animals that made up a chimera weren't really smart choices. In truth, snakes, lions, and goats hated each other, and it seemed strange to me that the mythical chimera didn't end up eating itself whole.

Meanwhile, the demon chimera I'd just defeated had since turned into a pile of ash. I looked down at it in curiosity, sniffing at the remains. "I thought magic couldn't kill a demon," I said to Aleam.

Aleam shook his head. "Not normal magic, no."

"Then why did this work? Because it looked to me it got destroyed by the shield."

"No," Ange said. "You did that, Ben. Your chimera strength backed it into a place where it had nowhere to go."

"You mean I crushed it."

"Like against a wall," Ange said. "You should have seen yourself,

Ben. You were so strong." She pretended to flex a bicep, and then giggled.

I raised my head, pride coursing through my mind. Rine went up to stand by Ange, and Lars went over to stand by Asinda. Seramina, meanwhile, was looking out at the flock of crows in the distance, tears in her eyes. Aleam had found a rock to sit down on, and he rested there, his breathing heavy.

I thought I should leave humans to do human things. So, instead, I went over to find Ta'ra in the army of Cat Sidhe. Part of me wanted to think that Astravar had done something terrible by casting this spell on all these fairies. But then he had also turned them into the greatest creature that had ever lived, and I was sure they'd see the benefits of being a cat soon.

Though they still didn't understand it, because the Cat Sidhe who hadn't yet turned into fairies did so one by one. They didn't take their glamour forms, but instead their golden floating specks floated across the sky, making everything look so pretty and pure. If they were anything like Ta'ra, then they could only transform eight times. Now, they were using their first transformation – probably because they couldn't yet accept who they'd actually become.

Soon, only two black cats with white diamond tufts on their chest remained. I stalked over to them, still with my head held high. One of them I knew just from her smell, it was Ta'ra and it was great to see her again.

Ta'ra turned to me, and she looked at me with her bright green eyes.

"Ben, I'm so sorry... I could see what I was doing. Although it was me when I led you to Faerini city, I thought I had control over myself. But I didn't realise that Astravar could seize my mind at any time."

"It's okay," I said, and I rubbed my face against hers. "Just let me have a little extra of your mackerel next time."

"Oh, so it was you that took it?"

"No... I wouldn't dare. You must have eaten it when possessed. Maybe Astravar was testing his connection to you or something."

Ta'ra looked off into the distance. "I guess." Then she turned to her companion. "By the way, did you ever meet Ta'lon?"

That was something I didn't want to hear. I turned to Ta'lon, and raised my back, hackles shooting out of it. "Ta'lon, your betrothed."

The male Cat Sidhe looked up at me. "Yes," he said. "What of it?"

"You cast her out of your society, and you were horrible to her. How do you think I would have felt if my humans just threw me out on the street?"

Ta'lon lowered his head. "It was years ago that I ordered Ta'ra evicted from our society. For many days since, I've regretted that decision from the bottom of my heart."

"You shouldn't have even done it in the first place," I said, growling at the prince.

"Ben, be civil," Ta'ra said. "And Ta'lon, before you get any smart ideas about fighting Ben, remember that he helped save your skin."

"And I'm a Bengal, descendant of the great Asian leopard cat," I pointed out. "I could probably teach you a thing or two about fighting. At least if I faced you at a fair size."

"I don't want to fight you," Ta'lon said. He yawned in a surprisingly cat-like way. "I'm still getting used to this... form."

"You soon will, and you'll realise it's the greatest form you can have," I said, lowering my back. This Ta'lon guy might have hurt Ta'ra, but otherwise he didn't seem all that bad. Although I still felt threatened by having another tomcat near Ta'ra.

"See what I mean," Salanraja said. *"You like her."* After Seramina had broken Astravar's spell, the dragons had since woke up and were

flying over to our location. They were getting closer now, so I could faintly hear Salanraja inside my mind.

"*Oh, shut up,*" I said.

"*Fine,*" Salanraja said. "*We're almost there now. I can't believe that I missed seeing you as a chimera.*"

"*And I hope you never get to see me that way again.*"

I looked over my shoulder to see that Aleam had lifted himself off his perch. He hobbled over, leaning on his staff and clutching the vial containing the yellow liquid in his free hand.

My heart sank. Whiskers, the cure, I'd completely forgotten about it. All this time to save Ta'ra, and now she'd probably drink the stuff with Ta'lon, and they'd go home together, and I would be a lonely cat in a strange land once again.

Ta'ra blinked at Aleam as he approached. "Is that the cure?"

Aleam looked at her, then at Ta'lon, then back at her again. "It is," he said. "I perfected it with a special ingredient."

"And what was that then?"

"Mandragora root. Enough to reverse the magic in one dose, I think. So long as you haven't used all of your nine transformations. But, unfortunately, there is only enough for one."

I purred and rubbed up against Ta'ra once again, feeling a little sad. "Are you going use it?"

Ta'ra didn't answer the question immediately, as she still had more she wanted to ask Aleam. "Mandragora. That only grows in the far reaches of the Darklands, right?"

"Ruled by the warlocks, with their magical conjurations guarding every mile, it is incredibly risky to obtain."

"And there's only enough for one dose, right?"

Aleam nodded slowly. "Unfortunately so."

"Then," Ta'ra said, turning to Ta'lon. "You should take it, Ta'lon."

"What? No? Ta'ra, I was fool enough to lose you once. I don't want to leave you again."

"But you will always have a place in my heart, my prince," Ta'ra said. "In a way, you were right to cast me out. The fairies would have never accepted me in this form, and it will take them a long time to accept the Cat Sidhe as they now are."

I don't know why, but Ta'ra's professions of affection for Ta'lon made my heart sink even more. Whiskers, it was almost as if I was becoming human. After I'd learned the language and tasted their magic, now I was feeling emotions a cat shouldn't feel.

Ta'lon lowered himself on his haunches. "Then what would you have me do?"

"Return home. Help your father and the other leaders in the Faerie Kingdoms understand that Cat Sidhe are not evil fae. We've not been corrupted, and we can live amongst them. They need to learn how to accept us."

"Or," Ta'lon said. "I can retrieve some Mandragora so that we can make more of the cure."

"No," Ta'ra rubbed her nose against Ta'lon's. "Ta'lon, you cannot fight the warlocks. They've become too strong, and they're becoming stronger. Please, do this for me."

Aleam uncorked the vial, and he approached Ta'lon with it. "Are you sure about this, Ta'ra?" he said. "I did develop it for you."

"I'm sure," Ta'ra said.

Aleam nodded, and he held out the vial towards Ta'lon. Ta'lon looked at Ta'ra with eyes even brighter and greener than hers. He paused a moment, then he lowered his head and approached the vial. Aleam tipped the liquid down the Cat Sidhe's throat, and then he took a step back.

A plume of golden smoke rose around Ta'lon. The cold wind soon blew this away, leaving a golden wisp that floated there for a moment, then glided away.

Ta'ra watched it go.

"What will you do now?" Aleam asked her.

"I'll wait here until the other Cat Sidhe turn back into cats again. Then, I'll help them set up a commune. They'll need to learn how to survive in this world. Because I feel it will be a long time before either we find a cure, or the fairies learn to accept us."

I mewled, sadly. "Can I come with you?" I asked. "I could be your teacher. Everyone can learn how to be a cat from me."

Aleam laughed. "I think you need to finish your studies at Dragonsbond Academy, Ben. But maybe when they've settled somewhere you can visit them."

"I guess," I said. "So, what happens next?"

"Well," Aleam said. "I'm just waiting for the king's guards to ride out of the city. I'm expecting they'll request an audience with us."

"You mean I'll get to meet a king?"

"You will," Aleam said, and he raised an eyebrow, probably because he caught the sarcasm in my voice.

"Big deal," I said. I honestly didn't get the whole monarchy thing. No one ruled over us cats and kept gold in treasuries and told us what to do. We just roamed the land as we pleased.

I turned to see Ange and Rine looking out towards the city. Rine had a hand on Ange's shoulder, and I wondered if this was finally a display of affection from him to her. But when Rine saw me looking at him, he retracted his hand, and his face went red.

Nearby, Prefect Asinda and Prefect Lars held hands, their staffs clutched in their free hands, with the bases resting against the ground and the crystals glowing red and white.

Seramina, meanwhile, sat on the rock where Aleam had been previously staring out into space. Her cheeks were wet with tears. I went over, thinking both that I could provide her comfort and she could provide me some too. I leapt up on her lap, and she reached down and stroked me, but she didn't look at me.

"So that's that then," she said. "I guess I'm truly alone."

I held that thought for a moment. Then I decided otherwise. "No," I said. "I don't think you are. None of us are."

That caused Seramina to look down at me. "How come?"

But I didn't need to answer that question, because from the direction of the Willowed Woods came a loud roar that cut apart the horizon. I remained silent, because Seramina knew, and I knew, and every one of us dragon riders present knew as we turned to face the seven dragons approaching over the horizon.

We would never be alone again because we had our dragons. And I guess I was starting to accept I'd be bonded to Salanraja for life.

EPILOGUE

D rat! Defeated by a cat again! I couldn't believe it. One time was injury, the second was insult. How could I, the mighty Astravar, let such a hopeless creature get in my way? The dragon rider teenagers were bad enough, but for a cat who used to be my minion to take up magic, destroy my beloved demon chimera, and stop me claiming the throne of Cimlean as my own... It caused hate to curdle in my mind.

Part of me wanted to reach out and taunt him using telepathic dark magic. But I couldn't bear the thought of his voice. I had to do something about him. If I couldn't destroy him alone, then I would get help. Anything to get him out of my path.

Then, there was my daughter. Many years ago, I might have felt sad about being rejected by her. But whenever even the slight hint of sadness emerged in me, I felt the magic coursing through my veins, and I remembered that guilt served no purpose in me anymore. Still, now I knew who she was I would have to find a way to convert her to my cause. All this, I would do in due time.

These were the thoughts milling around in my head, as I approached the floating platform. The dragon riders, I believed had their Council, and this was the location of the Council of the Warlocks. When, that was, we decided it necessary to meet. It must have been at least thirty years since we stood here last.

My crow kin had left me now, and I was flying alone as a crow above the beautiful magical mist that limned the Darklands. Right in the centre of this land hovered the platform on which we held these extremely rare councils. From the sky, it looked like a cog with seven long teeth. Seven crystals held the platform afloat high up in the clouds, each placed right underneath the teeth.

All seven of us had placed magical wards on our sides of the inner circle. To stand on any wards that weren't our own, or even to try and cross them by air would mean instant death. We also had our minions – stone golems – guarding the centre of the platform. We warlocks were paranoid, and I guess naturally so.

The glyph in the centre of one cog-tooth lit up as I flew down towards it. It displayed an image of a crow in flight, and this was the place I should stand. Here, I had to abide by the rules we'd all set. Do not try to cast magic. Do not raise my staff for any purpose whatsoever.

I was the first to arrive, and so I scanned the sky looking for the other warlocks. I'd summoned them through the magical ether – a spell we all knew how to cast and reserved for the most desperate of moments. We all favoured the ability to turn into birds that scavenge. I saw Cala first – a huge white seagull screeching into the air. She landed in her place opposite me, purple mist rising around her.

Her form when she emerged was of a beautiful red-haired woman. This one hadn't lost her looks, but then she'd used her magic to keep them. Junas came down next, a vulture. He was tall and lanky with a hooked nose and bald head. Then came Ritrad, the youngest of the warlocks. He was a buzzard, and his human form was giant and muscular. Lasinta took the condor form, and she was old and frail as a human. Moonz landed as a bald eagle. As a human he looked almost old as Lasinta, but of sturdier build. Finally came Pladana, a hawk. She was small and wiry as a human.

A moment of silence passed between us, as we let ourselves collect our thoughts. It lasted about a minute, before Lasinta called out. She was the oldest, and we'd decided she should always lead the council. Though, I hadn't really had much of a say in this matter.

"We haven't had a Council of the Warlocks for thirty years. What say you, Astravar?" Lasinta asked.

I explained the situation as succinctly as I could. I told the warlocks how Dragonsbond Academy was gaining power. How I'd found myself so close to defeating them, only to have been foiled by their new rising stars. I didn't mention one of them was a cat, nor did I mention another was my long-lost daughter. They didn't need to know those things.

The other six warlocks listened in silence. But I knew they weren't just listening; they were calculating. Working out exactly what I had to give, and how they could use this to gain magical power. I knew the game too well, which was why I was being extra careful not to give anything away.

After I'd finished, I took a deep breath, and we waited again in silence for someone to speak. Eventually, it was Moonz – the oldest male warlock, who'd landed as a hawk – who asked the question they all probably wanted to ask.

"What are you proposing? All you've given us so far is information. But I'm guessing you wouldn't have called us here without a plan."

I steepled my hands in glee. I hadn't thought it would be this easy to get them to listen. But no one yet had asked for anything to trade. They might have wanted crystals, or for me to hand over some of my minions to serve them.

"The dragon riders and the Kingdom of Cimlean are becoming too powerful. If we don't do something now, then they will eventually destroy us."

"Are you suggesting a war?" Moonz asked.

"That's exactly what I'm suggesting. All-out war. If we can combine our forces now, then we can defeat Dragonsbond Academy, and we can wipe out King Garmin's military. After that, we can decide amongst ourselves how to divide the spoils."

Another long silence ensued. I'd delivered the last line on purpose, because everyone here knew what it meant. We would unite to kill our common enemies, then we would turn amongst each other and battle amongst ourselves.

But clearly, given that the cat's destiny and mine were intertwined, I didn't have the power to defeat it. These warlocks were independent from that destiny, and so any of them could sever the link between me and the cat.

"We shall put it to the vote," Lasinta said. "Raise your staff and light it if you want to go to war."

I raised mine immediately to show that I was fully behind my plan. It lit up with a bright purple light, emitting a beam into the clouds above. Pladana raised hers next, and then Cala. Junas, and Ritrad followed. Moonz then raised his, and Lasinta raised hers last.

Soon, seven lights shone up into the sky – beacons for all of our minions down on the surface to see.

"It is so," Lasinta called out.

"Good," I said, as we all lowered our staffs together. "Then I suggest that we take stock of our inventories and then meet back here in three days to discuss our plans."

I didn't wait for an answer. I wanted to show them that I had things to do. So, I let the purple mist rise around me, breathing in its cold, heady scent. I was soon a crow, flying into the Darklands, cawing out my victory to the world.

Finally, the time to destroy the kingdom and start my conquest of the seven dimensions was nigh.

ACKNOWLEDGEMENTS

MANY PEOPLE HELPED ME in bringing this novel to fruition, and I'm immensely grateful to everyone who did.

Firstly, I'd like to thank Wayne M. Scace for your hard work editing the manuscript. Thank you, Wayne for your invaluable help and flexibility working with me chapter by chapter to help alleviate those tight deadlines.

Thank you, also, for Carol Brandon, for the scrupulous proof-reading work. I really do appreciate your flexibility working with me despite the tight deadlines, as well as your patience about the delays.

A massive shout out to my ARC team, who have been incredibly supportive in reading, providing feedback, and leaving wonderful reviews. Thank you also to every reader of this book, the one that came before it, and my other works. I appreciate everything that you do to support the world of publishing and literature at large.

Thank you also to those readers who helped with the typo hunting in the final draft, including Tsippi Jelingold.

I'd finally like to thank my family. Particularly my wife Ola who provided an immense amount of help reading and re-reading this story. A huge thank you to my parents as well for all the support they have given me throughout my writing career.

Thank you for reading "*A Cat's Guide to Meddling With Magic*". I hope that you enjoyed it and that it added value for you in your every day life.

I have written a prequel novelette to this novel entitled "*A Cat's Guide to Serving a Warlock*", which you can download for free by signing up to my newsletter at https://chrisbehrsin.com/servingawarlock.

I send bi-monthly emails with promos, giveaways, information about new releases and news about what's going on in my life in general.

Once again, the cat must save the day

Ben who rides dragons is twice a hero. He's defeated all kinds of demons and learned how to transform into a chimera. That's powerful stuff for a mere cat. Oh, how proud his ancestors would be if they saw him today ...

In fact, he's far too powerful for Astravar, the mighty warlock and Ben's nemesis, who can't stand the thought of being defeated by a mere moggie. But now he has allied with the other warlocks and together they have a plan to destroy the kingdom.

Obviously, when the warlocks attack, everyone's going to turn to the mighty Dragoncat for help. That's the problem with being a hero, you see. When threats loom on the horizon, everyone expects said hero to step up to the plate and save the day.

Alas, war involves giving up a lot of home comforts, and Ben doesn't like that one bit.

"A CAT'S GUIDE TO SAVING THE KINGDOM" is the third book in the first Dragoncat trilogy – a series of fun and kid-friendly dragon riding adventures where not only humans befriend dragons, but cats (and a dog) too.

AVAILABLE AT MAJOR RETAILERS

Made in United States
Troutdale, OR
05/15/2024

19882843R10152